# Wendy's Pirate

USA TODAY BESTSELLING AUTHOR

## ERIN BEDFORD

# Also by Erin Bedford

**The Underground Series**
Chasing Rabbits
Chasing Cats
Chasing Princes
Chasing Shadows
Chasing Hearts
The Crimes of Alice
Hatter's Heart
Cheshire's Smile

**The Mary Wiles Chronicles**
Marked by Hell
Bound by Hell
Deceived by Hell
Tempted by Hell

**Starcrossed Dragons**
Riding Lightning
Grinding Frost
Swallowing Fire
Pounding Earth

**The Crimson Fold**
Until Midnight
Until Dawn
Until Sunset

**Curse of the Fairy Tales**
Rapunzel Untamed
Rapunzel Unveiled
Rapunzel Unchained

**Her Angels**
Heaven's Embrace
Heaven's A Beach
Heaven's Most Wanted

**House of Durand**

Indebted to the Vampires
Wanted by the Vampires
Protected by the Vampires
Embrace of the Vampires
Tempted by the Butler
Loved by the Vampires
Huntress of the Vampires

**<u>Academy of Witches</u>**
Witching On A Star
As You Witch
Witch You Were Here
Just Witch It
Summer Witchin'

**<u>Children of the Fallen</u>**
Death In Her Eyes
Fire In Her Blood

**<u>House of Van Helsing</u>**
Her Cross To Bear

**<u>Fairy Tale Bad Boys</u>**
Beauty and the Hunter
Wendy's Pirate


The Beast of the Fae Court
Granting Her Wish
Vampire CEO

USA TODAY BESTSELLING AUTHOR

# ERIN BEDFORD

# CHAPTER 1
## *WENDY*

SHE HATED THE color blue. Not just any blue but cerulean blue. The blue that every kid in the class wanted to play with. The same color blue as Wendy's no-good man-whore of an ex-boyfriend's eyes. Unfortunately, it was also the color of the ocean that rolled beneath the ship carrying her from Florida to the newly opened Fae resort, Never Isles.

When the supernatural world decided to come out of their perpetual closet, a whole array of new places seemed to pop up out of nowhere. The lost city of Atlantis? Yeah, not so lost anymore when it appeared in the middle of the Gulf of Mexico, teaming with merpeople who could switch between human and mermaid at a whim.

So, it shouldn't have been a surprise when smack dab in the middle of the Bermuda Triangle, an Island appeared with hundreds of Fae pouring out of it. Now advertised as a resort, it was the destination spot for those looking for a getaway from mundane adult life. Considering what she left behind in New York, Wendy needed a gateway more than anyone else.

Growing up had never been hard for Wendy. Especially not with her family in England, where she'd been expected to be mature and know how to behave. It was no surprise that at the age of nine she'd known she wanted to be a lawyer. Something about being in front of all of those people defending someone else's honor set right with her. So, twenty years later, after almost a decade of school, she had fulfilled that goal by landing a respectable junior associate at Darling and Darling, L.L.P.

The law firm was run by the two sons of the Darling clan, and Wendy had instantly been drawn to Michael, the younger one. Against her better judgment, she'd started a secret relationship with him. The company had a strict no fraternization policy, but Michael had assured her that it would be fine, as long as they kept it quiet. She'd trusted him; that was, until she'd walked in on him and a big-busted dark haired beauty in the copy room.

Now, all Wendy wanted was to forget about him and New York. The best way to do that was a fun-filled week of nothing but relaxation and maybe even a bit of naughtiness, if she found the right guy.

"Miss?" A voice sounded from her side, pulling her eyes away from the waters and to the sailor's pinched face. "We are coming up on port now, make sure you have all your belongings, and I suggest standing back from the railing."

"Of course. Thank you." Wendy nodded her head and tucked the chestnut colored hair that blew over her face behind her ear. Sighing, her light brown eyes glanced toward the approaching emerald green trees of the island.

If she did find someone to make her forget about Michael, it would be for fun only. No more relationships for her. At least not for a while. After up and quitting her first real job as a lawyer, she needed to refresh and recharge. Then she would be ready for anything those sniping New York lawyers could throw at her.

STEPPING OFF THE platform and onto solid ground, Wendy's eyes widened as she scanned the area before her.

Many different images had crossed her mind when she'd decided to come to the Never Isles, but none of them could have prepared her for the completely and utterly boring port market.

There were vendors set up along the coast, each trying to peddle their wares to the passing tourists. The island must have been bigger than she'd thought, because there were taxis lined up, waiting to take passengers to their destinations. Wendy wouldn't be needing any of them, because she was staying on the seafront. In all honesty, she was a bit put off by the lack of difference from any other resort she had been to.

Where were the supernatural creatures? The magic and the wow? She couldn't see any of the promised panty-wetting fae, or the promise of instant relaxation she was supposed to feel the moment she stepped on the island. If anything she was tenser than before.

"Want your picture taken?" A man came up to her and the camera flashed in her eyes, causing spots to fill her vision before she could say no.

"No thank you," she grumbled as she covered her eyes and shifted to move away from the man.

Finding a bench next to the docking station, Wendy tried to get her bearings. Nothing was going as planned, and she was regretting coming here at all.

"Maybe I should just go home," she muttered to herself, holding her bags against her chest like a security blanket.

"Don't do that. You just got here." A panty-melting masculine voice filled her ears, causing an instant ache to start between her thighs.

Wendy turned toward the direction the voice had come from, and the ache turned into an all-out waterfall. His auburn hair was tousled, as if he had been playing in the wind all day, and his dark green eyes were alight with mischief. The smile he was giving her promised all kinds of naughty adventures if she would just say yes.

"And why shouldn't I?" Wendy cleared her throat when it came out as a croak rather than a question. "This isn't exactly what I paid for."

"It isn't?" His slim but muscular figure sat beside her on the bench. He placed an arm around the back of the bench the heat from his proximity making her blush.

"No, it's not." She should have moved away from him. Just because he was hot, and caused all kinds of delicious thoughts to run through her mind, didn't mean she could trust him. But the more she tried to make herself move away, the more she wanted to be near him. What was he?

He turned his body toward her and picked up a lock of hair that had fallen out of her bun, fingering the ends of it as if he were running his fingertip up and down her thigh. The reaction was the same as before, causing her legs to press together in need.

"I think you were expecting magic and excitement. To be in a constant state of awe for the world around you. Am I wrong?" He asked the question while looking up from beneath thick eyelashes, making the boyish side of him stand out more.

Wendy nodded her head in agreement.

"Well." The mysterious man dropped her hair and crossed one leg over the other, looking out around them. "You won't find any of that here at the port."

"I won't?"

"No, but I know where you can find it." He smirked at her and stood from his seat, stretching his arms above his head. Wendy watched the ripple of muscles beneath his dark t-shirt and jeans. If she hadn't already been attracted to him, his fabulous ass would have sealed the deal for her. She could never say no to a man that looked that good in a pair of pants. It was probably why she'd ended up with Michael in the first place.

The thought of Michael caused her to frown. She was supposed to be forgetting about him, not comparing every guy she met to him.

"Now, what's with the sad face?" The man turned to her, his hands on his hips. "You aren't having fun yet? Well, we'll have to fix that. Come on."

He held his hand out to her and Wendy stopped herself from instantly taking it. What was wrong with her? She wasn't this impulsive. She thought things through, made lists, and weighed all the options. Wendy was not one to go with a guy just because he asked her.

"I don't even know you. Why should I come with you?" Wendy was proud that her voice came out a bit haughty rather than breathless from how turned on she was.

Frowning at her, he cocked his head to the side. "You don't know me?" He asked the question like it was the most ludicrous thing he'd ever heard, which made her even more suspicious of his intentions.

"No, I don't. Now if you don't mind." Wendy felt her spine finally solidify back into place, and she stood from the bench coming nose to nose with him. "I need to check into my ro … room…"

Her words trailed off as her senses took in his scent. She hadn't noticed the spicy sandalwood smell before, but now it filled her head, making her lightheaded and a bit giddy. Before she could stop it, a smile spread across her face, and she couldn't think of anything she'd rather do than go with this man. Who cared who he was, he was there and he would make sure she had a great time.

"That's better." The man placed an arm around her waist and ushered her down the boardwalk.

Leaning her head on his shoulder she sighed in contentment. "I never do this, you know. I don't even know you name."

The man chuckled, the movement causing a rumble in his chest that vibrated through her and straight to her core.

"You can call me Peter. Peter Pan."

# CHAPTER 2
## *JAMES*

IT WAS GOOD to be back. Though, James had technically only been gone for a few hours, in the Never Isles a few hours was equivalent to a few days. After living on the island for the last two decades, James' internal clock had adjusted to the fast pace of the fae realm, making the human realm seem never-ending.

The moment James saw that glittering mountain peak and the vivid green of the surrounding forest, his body felt a hundred times lighter. He always felt as if he was floating on air when he made the transition between the human and fae realm. The thin layer of magic that separated the two realms probably had something to do with it.

When the Never Isles first appeared in the middle of the Caribbean, the surrounding lands were in a state of panic. Naval ships and fighter planes hovered around the edges, not sure of what to make of the new island surrounded by a sparkling bubble of magic.

The government had their best people on the job and even employed a few witches to try and make sense of the phenomenon. James was one of those people. He was one of the first to go through the bubble of magic and have that lighter than air feeling. He had yet to feel anything better than that.

He loved his life on the island and once he was forced out of the military, he fought to find his way back there. To where he felt safe. Where he belonged.

If only *he* wasn't there.

James' dark eyes searched out the port from the bow of his ship, looking for that familiar copper head of hair. It was easy to track the fae down. James only had to look as far as the most attractive woman on the tourist trap.

When he spotted *him*, James' eyes instantly latched onto the woman he was putting the moves on. She was a pretty little thing. Light brown hair, a sweet nose, and lips that even bowed down in a frown, causing his cock to stir. But that damn fae was working his magic on her. She didn't deserve that. None of the women who came to the Island did.

Most of the tourist were overworked Americans who were just looking for a bit of fun before heading back to the day-to-day grind. They wanted to get drunk and get fucked. The fae were experts in both areas. Especially Peter Pan.

Using their powers against humans was strictly forbidden. It was part of the treaty they'd signed when they'd opened the resort. The Council of Supernatural Creatures was merciless to those who opposed their laws. Unfortunately, Pan was part of that council, and it was near impossible to get any kind of proof that he was breaking the very laws he was supposed to enforce. When approached about it, he denied all allegations, claiming he was just that irresistible.

James snorted. Yeah, and he would grow a hook for a hand.

A smile crept up his face when the woman seemed to come to her senses, just as Pan tried to coax her to come with him. The look of befuddlement on the fae's face was almost good enough to make James forget about the shitty day he'd had; almost. When the woman stood up and was once again under the spineless fiend's spell, James' grin dissolved. He waited to see if she would snap out of it again but she didn't; she let herself be led away.

"Shit." He cursed under his breath and stepped toward the ramp leading off his ship and toward the dock.

"Uh, Capt'n." The timid voice of his first mate stopped him in his tracks.

"What is it, Smith?" James turned on the smaller man with a growl.

Taylor Smith was a short, stocky man in his late 50's who seemed to be more suited for desk work than as his first mate. James couldn't deny that while Smith was lacking in many ways, he was the best first mate he ever had, even if he was worse than a mouse.

"You wanted me to let you know when the shipment had been unloaded," Smith stuttered over his words, his hands shaking as he held his pen and clipboard in front of him.

"And?"

"And what, Capt'n?" His eyes widened underneath his bushy eyebrows, making them look like two caterpillars sitting on top of balls.

Groaning his frustration, James wiped a hand down his face. "Has the shipment been unloaded?"

"Oh, yes!" Smith rushed to answer. "They just finished. Everything went according to plan."

"Fine. Then tell the men they are free to go home for the evening." James waved a hand at Smith, his eyes turning back to the coast, searching for the copper head of hair, but couldn't see him anywhere.

Smith waited at his side and then cleared his throat.

"What now?" James snarled, giving up on finding the fae.

"There's one more thing, I thought you ought to know about." Smith gripped his pen so hard his knuckles turned white, and James made his face soften a bit. He really was too hard on the man.

"All right, what is it?"

If anything Smith seemed more anxious than before as James watched him fight to find his words.

"Come on, Smith. I don't have all day." He sighed and headed toward his office onboard the ship.

The sound of Smith's feet padding after him was accompanied by a muttered sentence that brought James to a screeching halt.

Spinning on the man, James' face filled with horror. "What did you say?"

"I ... I said that some men were asking after you back at the mainland." Smith backed away from James as if he were a crocodile planning to eat him.

"And what did they ask?" His heartbeat sped up and a feeling of panic clogged his throat as he waited for the answer.

"They didn't say. Just wanting to know if this ship was being run by James Clocker and where could they find him." Smith's shoulder drew back, and he stood taller. "I told them that the ship was run by the best captain this side of the Caribbean, and that if they had business with him they could go through the Council."

James smiled at the man's backbone, a feeling of relief washing through him.

Clapping a hand on Smith's shoulder, James chuckled. "Good work, Smith. You know just what to say to get those idiots from the military off my trail. I'm assuming they were military, correct?"

Smith's shoulders sagged and he nodded his head. "Yes, Capt'n. They had naval uniforms on and everything."

"Great." James turned back to his office door and then paused. "And Smith."

"Yes?"

"Be sure to keep an eye out for any more of those kinds of inquiries, on the Island and on the mainland. Wouldn't do to have them sneak up on us in our own back yard now would it?"

"Of course, Capt'n. I'll be sure to let the crew know as well." Smith nodded his head and made his way to what only James could assume was his home.

Opening his office door, James threw his coat off and plopped down in his chair. Pouring himself a tumbler of scotch, he sighed.

He had thought, when he moved to the Never Isles, that the military would lay off him. Fifteen years and they were still trying to hunt his ass down for a crime he hadn't even committed. He would have to be on his guard now more than ever, and that meant no more getting involved with things that weren't his business.

He forced all thoughts of rescuing one more innocent woman from that prick Pan out of his mind. James had his own survival to worry about. He just hoped the woman had a strong enough head on her shoulders to keep that fae out of her mind and from between her legs.

# CHAPTER 3
## *WENDY*

WIND BLOWING IN her face, Wendy chased after the fae called Peter Pan. Her lungs burned from the excessive running. Growling at herself for falling so far behind, she promised she'd start taking that spin class again, even if it was at an ungodly hour.

"Come on, Wendy. Keep up," Peter called out behind him as he darted between the trees of the island.

Pausing to catch her breath, Wendy placed a hand on the nearest tree. What had possessed her to agree to a run in the woods anyways? She wasn't a woods kind of girl. Hell, she wasn't an outdoors kind of girl. Wendy was perfectly happy sitting at home watching telly or going out for a drink, not tracking through the woods in near darkness.

But she knew what had gotten into her. It was Peter. All he had to do was blink those pretty green eyes of his and all of her excuses melted away.

The throbbing between her legs had been a consistent ache since meeting the fae, and she was beginning to wonder if it was some kind of magic, rather than her uncontrollable hormones. She was a respectable lawyer for Christ's sake, not some horny teenager.

He had somehow liquefied her insides so completely that she would do anything for him at the drop of a hat. And he hadn't even kissed her yet!

What was she doing in the middle of the forest with a man she'd just met? Something in the back of her mind told her this wasn't right. She shouldn't be here. Her heart raced and her eyes searched around her as a panic began to close in. Wendy was getting ready to bolt, and then *his* voice filled her ears.

"What are you doing?"

The sound of it vanquished any thoughts of running away, and the terror inside of her flittered off into the breeze, replaced by a throbbing that demanded her to stay close to him.

"Oh, you know, just enjoying the night air," Wendy lied, giving Peter a sultry smile.

He returned her smile with an electrifying one of his own that soared straight through Wendy and right to her aching core.

Leaning an arm on either side of the tree she was using as support, he blocked her in, his face coming inches from her mouth. Wendy's breath caught and her eyes locked onto his lips closing in on her.

"We could enjoy it together," Peter whispered against her lips before capturing them with his.

Wendy sighed into the kiss, a part of her able to breathe now that he had finally touched her. The kiss wasn't enough, though, it seemed the more he kissed her; the more she wanted him in return. So much so that she wrapped her arms around him, pulling him down to her. A chuckle rumbled through his chest. He slipped his arms around her waist, her body catching on fire where his pressed up against hers.

He slid a hand down her leg and hitched it over his hip, grinding his length against her center. She gasped out loud at the contact to her clit, her head falling back in ecstasy. Peter rotated his hips against her. The fabric of her pants rubbed against her, bringing her closer to that peak that had been out of reach all day.

When he pulled back from her, dropping her leg, she nearly cried. Bloody hell! She was almost there.

"Why'd you stop?" she croaked out, forcing herself not to beg him to finish what he'd started.

Brushing a hand along her face, Peter smiled, a mischievous glint in his eyes. "While I'd like nothing more than to fuck you against this tree, we have people waiting for us, and it would be rude to keep them waiting."

Wendy's lower lip stuck out in a pout, but she shook it off when Peter grabbed her hand in his and began to lead her back through the forest.

As before, Wendy was having a hard time keeping up with the fae and found herself tripping over her own feet. Eventually, Peter seemed frustrated with her lagging behind because he stopped and gave an exasperated sigh before lifting her up into his arms and carrying her to their destination. A destination that she had hoped to stay away from.

The tourist strip.

"What are we doing back here?" She scanned the crowded coast, taking in the various tourists partying and generally having a good time. When she had followed the fae into the woods, she'd thought they were going to a secret party, or maybe getting naughty in the woods, but to only end up back on the strip after she almost broke her ankle didn't make any sense.

"I thought you said we were going to have some fun. This ..." She gestured at the crowd. "... is not what I'd call fun."

"Relax." Peter smirked, waving her off. "I said we were going to have fun and we are." He grasped her chin in his hand, his green eyes mesmerizing her. "Don't you trust me?"

"Of course." Her voice came out breathless and needy as she drowned in the depths of his scent.

"Good, then let's go." He dropped his hand from her face and made his way through the crowd not looking back to see if she was following him.

Shaking the haze from her head, she hurried after his retreating form. Part of her wondered how she'd gotten talked into following a man she didn't know around, while the other half was too busy staring at Peter's delicious backside.

When Peter finally stopped, they were on one of the docks, next to a ship called the Jolly Roger. Her brow furrowed where Peter stood with four other men behind a stack of crates. They were all equally as attractive, but with less of a commanding presence. They clapped Peter on the back when he came over, their voices too low for her to make out what they were saying.

Wendy approached the fae with cautious steps, her eyes scanned around her, watching for anyone that would draw attention to their little group. But no one seemed to pay them any mind. In fact, those who did see them quickly turned the other way, as if they didn't want to be involved. At the back of her mind, Wendy thought it was strange, but as soon as Peter's voice resonated, she couldn't bring herself to care.

"Hey, Wendy!" Peter called out to her waving her over. "I want you to meet some of my friends."

Stopping next to him, Wendy gave a small wave, unsure of what she was supposed to do. "Hello."

"Man, Pete. You really knocked it out of the park with this one. I'm Bear, by the way, sweetheart. And you can come cuddle with me anytime." One of the guys leered at her chest, and Wendy forced herself not to cross her arms. In her experience, the more you acted like it bothered you, the more they would do it. Ignoring them seemed to knock the wind out of their sails.

"I know, right?" Peter chuckled, not caring about his friend's disgusting display. He wrapped an arm around her waist, pulling her close to his side.

Wendy snuggled in, gazing up at him with longing. She couldn't wait to get this over with so they could finally be alone. Her body told her she couldn't wait much longer before she jumped him, the audience be damned.

"So, what are we doing here?" Her eyes locked onto the Jolly Roger and then went back to Peter, her face full of curiosity.

The men around her chuckled, the sound of it caused a tingle to zip through her. Were all the fae men like this? Or was it just her?

"You see that ship there?" Peter pointed a finger at the ship they were next to and she nodded. It was hard not to notice it. "A really bad human owns it, and we want to get proof that he is here so the authorities will come take him away."

"But why don't you just tell the authorities he is here in the first place?" Wendy cocked her head to the side.

"Don't you think we've tried that?" One of the other men scoffed. "They won't give us the time of day unless we have proof. As far as they are concerned, he is a law abiding citizen who has done nothing but help us." The fae spat on the ground and Wendy's lip curled up as she tried not to gag.

Disgusting.

"Look, babe." Peter turned her in his arms, his hands on her shoulders. "We need to get something out of there that proves he's a wanted criminal. Which he is," Peter hurried to add.

Wendy nodded. As a lawyer, she knew that most of the time, the local police wouldn't take your word for it without some kind of substantial evidence. Evidence that usually wasn't given over so freely.

"None of us have been able to sneak in without getting caught. But you ..." his eyes trailed over her form, causing her body to heat, "... you are the perfect size to wiggle through one of those portholes. So, what do you say? Will you help me rid our island of a fugitive?" Peter's hands slid down to her hips and pulled her flush against his body, letting her feel his hardened length against her stomach.

Insides clenching in need, Wendy felt like a bobble head with how fast she agreed to his bidding.

"Great." The one called Bear clapped his hands together. "Now that it's settled, let's get moving. We don't know when that bastard will show up again."

Directing Wendy toward one of the port holes, Peter helped boost her up so she could reach the window.

Her hands pushed on the glass, hoping that it was locked so she and Peter could just go back to her hotel room and forget about all this, she groaned inwardly as the window creaked open.

Poking her head inside, she searched around the darkened room. The moon didn't do much to help her see anything. She pulled back and looked down at Peter who was smiling like an idiot with his hands full of her arse.

"Well?" one of the men whispered from behind her. "What are you waiting for?"

Wendy scowled at them and stuck her head back in the window, before using her arms to pull the rest of her body through and onto a desk full of charts and graphs. Climbing over them, she tried to make as little noise as possible.

When her feet landed on the floor, she turned about the room. As her eyes adjusted to the darkness she began to notice different parts of the room. It seemed like some sort of office with its large desk and a bookshelf that made her drool.

*Snap out of it, Wendy. You've got a job to do.* Shaking her head, she lifted a few papers looking for anything that would point to the owner being a criminal.

While usually, she didn't go around breaking and entering, especially not for law related scenarios, she was all for getting justice on a broken system. A lawyer she may be, but that didn't mean she was blind to the holes in the system. Too many times good men and women were put behind bars for crimes they didn't commit while the real culprits walked free. It was one reason she had decided to be a defense lawyer.

Picking up a book off the bookshelf, Wendy opened it to find shipping logs. They didn't look suspicious, especially out in the open, but they might help Peter find something. She tucked the book under her arm and kept searching.

After a few minutes of not finding anything remotely looking like the owner was anything other than a normal merchant captain, she turned back to the window with her book of logs in her hand. Climbing back up onto the table, she was just about to get out the window when the door of the office slammed open.

"You there! Stop." A deep voice rumbled and Wendy scrambled to get to the window.

Getting her head out, she looked down to where Peter had been, only to find him and his friends gone. She didn't have the chance to contemplate jumping before she was jerked away from the hole and came face to face with what had to be the ship's captain.

# CHAPTER 4
## *JAMES*

A LUCKY BASTARD, that's what he was. James had expected Pan and his men to come sniffing around his ship eventually. They'd done it before. This time, though, they'd used the human woman he'd seen Pan with earlier.

When James had heard movement in the ship from his bedroom, he'd been prepared for a fight. But he never expected to come face to ass with the petite brunette from the coast. He'd let himself be distracted by her lovely backside until he noticed his ledger book in her hands.

That wouldn't do.

Hands wrapped around her waist, he easily picked her up and away from the window. She fought against him as he threw her over his shoulder. She cried out as her small hands beat at his back before he dumped her onto the couch.

"Unhand me, you bloody brute." Her eyes flung daggers at him, while her hair had fallen in disarray around her face. Making her even more beautiful than she'd been before.

"Ah, a Brit. What are you doing on our side of the pond?" He started conversationally, hoping to win her over with sweet talk.

"None of your business." The brunette sniffed, turning her head away.

"Well, now how 'bout a name then?" Seeing she wasn't going to answer, James continued, "Mine is James. James Clocker and you are aboard my lovely Jolly Roger."

"That's a stupid name for a ship." She scoffed.

Ignoring her comment, James paced in front of her. "It was named after my bunk mate Rogers who, God help him, wouldn't stop being so damn happy all the time. And thus he was from then on known as Jolly Roger."

"But why would you name your ship after him?" Her eyes seemed eager to absorb, and it made him wonder what else would make her eager.

"He died in a mission gone bad, but ole Roger was happy up until he passed away. Right in my arms." James looked down at his arms, a frown marred his face.

"Really?" The woman gasped, a hand going up to her mouth.

"Nope, not really." James tucked his hands in his pockets and laughed. "Now I've told you about me, who are you?"

"Wendy," she huffed. "My name is Wendy. Now, will you let me go?"

"Not yet. I have to figure out what to do with you first." James smiled to himself. Wendy. That was the kind of name he thought she would have. Something light and flowy, just like her.

Brow scrunched down as she took in his words, she sat back on the couch. In her silence, James took the moment to look her over. He hadn't been able to see her very well on the tourist trap, but now with her sitting before him, a pout on her lips, it took everything in him not to take her right there.

Her light brown eyes that matched the same exact shade as her hair were so fierce with her hatred of him, that James felt himself hardening. This wasn't good.

Turning from the tempting minx, James made his way over to his desk. Plopping down in his chair, he propped up his feet and watched her. And waited.

After a moment or so, he could see her getting frustrated with his silence, causing a smirk to climb up his face.

"Well?" She growled at him, in a voice that made him wonder if she sounded the same while in the throes of passion. He'd bet she liked to bite and claw. The thought of it made him shiver in delight. He really hoped he'd get the chance to find out.

"Well, what?" He responded to her question with a question.

"Aren't you going to call the police? I've broken into your home and have stolen your property." She held up the book in her hand.

"No, you haven't." James shook his head and smiled at her frown. "This." He gestured around him. "Is not my home, it's my work. And you haven't stolen anything since you aren't going anywhere."

Hot rage covered her face as she realized what he said. Watching the play of emotion on her features was better than drinking himself into a stupor any day.

"You can't keep me here. I'm a lawyer. I know my rights!" Her voice screeched into hysteria that made his ears ring.

"A lawyer, huh?" James dropped his feet to the ground, his hard-on no longer prominent after the abuse to his ears, and made his way toward her. Dark eyes locked onto almond brown.

"Yes." Confidence rang through her voice and she matched his stare with one of her own. "And if you do not let me go, I will see that you are charged with kidnapping."

"And this is before or after you admit how you got here in the first place?" James chuckled as her mouth opened and shut before she growled once more.

"Look, I didn't even want to be here. So here." She shoved the book at him as she stood up. "Take this back, and we can forget this ever happened."

Taking the book from her hands, James tossed it to the side. "Thank you, but that's not good enough."

"What? I gave you your stupid book back. Now let me go. There is no reason for you to keep me here." The woman came toe to toe with him, shoving her finger at his chest.

"Actually, I don't need a reason to keep you here, but let's just say it's punishment for giving into peer pressure." James stood tall, letting his size do all his intimidating for him. At six-four, he was a foot or more taller than her, and he would bet his arm was thicker than her waist.

"Peer pressure? I wasn't doing it for my friends."

"Ah. Then it must be because of a man then, isn't it?" James clucked his tongue when her face softened, and a glaze covered her eyes. Just as he thought. "You shouldn't change yourself for a man. It'll only end in heartbreak."

"What do you know? Do you even have a heart?" She pushed her finger even harder into his chest, causing him to wince.

"Of course I don't, but that doesn't mean I don't want to save yours." Grabbing onto the offending hand, he dragged her over to a drawer in the bookshelf along the wall. Opening it, he dug around until his fingers found the cool metal of the handcuffs.

When her eyes landed on them, she began to scream and fight him as he maneuvered her back to the couch. If she had been a bit bigger, and if he didn't have military training, she probably would have gotten away. As it was, all it did was end with her back on the couch and James hovering on top of her.

"What the fuck do you think you're doing?" she screeched, her legs trying to kick him off, but he pressed his lower half against her so she wouldn't hit him in the jewels.

"Saving you from yourself," he muttered leaning down until their faces were mere inches apart. He almost gave in and took her lips in his when she gasped. Instead, he forced himself to lean down toward the ground, snapping the one end of the cuff to the bottom of the couch and then the other around her wrist.

Getting up from the couch, he watched her struggle against the metal. Her small form prone on the lumpy piece of furniture that he knew wasn't at all comfortable to sleep on. But he couldn't have her near him, or he'd be no better than Pan.

"You can't do this!" She pulled her arm, but he knew she wasn't strong enough to break the chain. Those were military grade. If they wanted you to stay put, that was what you were going to do.

"Actually, I can. You're not yourself right now." James made his way to the door, flicking the light off. "You'll thank me in the morning. Have a good night." The door closed behind him barely muffling the protests of his captive.

With a heavy sigh, James made his way back to his room and far away from the tempting woman on his couch. He wasn't a bad guy, but he couldn't let her go yet. Not with Pan's magic still in her system. He knew from experience that the moment he let her go, she'd dart back to him like a cat in heat.

She needed time to cool her head and realize what had happened. Then maybe she'd be singing a different tune. Then maybe he could get the proof he needed against the rapist bastard and keep his own head out of hot water while doing it.

# CHAPTER 5
## *WENDY*

WHEN WENDY WOKE the next morning, her arm ached and her mouth tasted like something had died in it. Cracking open her eyes, she thanked all that was holy that the only window in the office was the tiny porthole she had come through last night.

Last night. "Ugh." She groaned, burying her face in the couch. What had possessed her to break into someone's property? Then she remembered what James had said.

She wasn't herself.

That was true. The moment she'd stepped on the island she'd felt ill at ease. Then she'd been approached by Peter, and all of her caution seemed to have gone out the window as if by magic.

Her stomach rolled, and she felt like she was going to hurl. How had she been so stupid? She had seen enough cases of magically influenced relationships to know when she was being controlled.

Peter was attractive, she would give him that, but there was no way possible she would have just up and went with him if she'd been in her right mind. People didn't do that. *She* didn't do that.

Jerking up for the couch, her whole body felt violated. The places she had let him touch her, how she had begged him to fuck her in the woods. Everything was just wrong.

Both hands pulled at her hair as she agonized over the last twenty-four hours. What was she going to do? Could she press charges? She didn't really have any proof but her word against his, unless she could get the captain to testify against him.

The captain. Captain James Clocker was one hell of a male specimen. Pitch black hair, dark eyes that seared through her. Just the thought of his large shoulders and square jaw made her weak in the knees. If she hadn't been under Peter's influence, she would have creamed her pants right then and there.

One thing she could thank the fae for, not that she would. The only time she would be thanking him would be when he was being led away in handcuffs, and her place back in the courtroom was secured.

Thinking of handcuffs made her suddenly remember hers. Or the absence of them. Looking down at her wrist, she frowned when she saw the cuff still there, but no longer attached to the couch. No wonder she had forgotten all about it.

Next to her feet, she noticed a shiny key, a cup of coffee, and a note. Ignoring the key and note she grabbed the coffee in her hands and drank it down. It was barely lukewarm, meaning that James must have been here recently. Lukewarm or not, the man knew how to make a cup of coffee.

With the lack of suitable tea choices in America, Wendy had quickly joined the coffee addicts that lined up outside Starbucks. The fact that the captain had provided her with her daily dose made her forgive him a bit for locking her up. Just a bit.

Coffee drunk, she placed the cup down on the side table and grabbed the key from the floor. She stuck the key in the lock at her wrist, clicking it with a sigh. Rubbing her wrist, she glanced back to the floor where the remaining item sat.

Brow crinkled, she reached down and picked up the note. She half expected him to tell her he was suing her for breaking and entering as well as stealing. Or at least chastise her more about Peter. But the note was actually friendly....ish.

*Wendy,*

*I had to head out for an early meeting. I know the coffee is not English Breakfast Tea but it works in a pinch.*

*I hope you have come to your senses by now and realize what Pan has done to you is wrong. If you would like to press charges I am available anytime.*

*I'm sure it goes without saying but STAY AWAY FROM PAN. If not I will have to go to extreme measures and I can't promise that the next time I have you tied up I will be able to restrain myself.*

*J*

Wendy gulped. The thought of having the dark-haired captain tying her up made her a bit more excited than it should have. She remembered what it felt like to have him pressed against her when he was putting the cuffs on, and even through her magical haze, part of her had wanted him.

Putting the note down, Wendy stood from the couch and made her way to the door. She placed her hand on the knob, half expecting it to be locked, but it turned with ease.

Out in the corridor, she looked down both sides of the hall, trying to figure out where to go. The sound of people working came from her right, so Wendy turned toward it. She passed a few men dressed in work clothes; a few of them gave her curious looks, but went about their business.

When she finally got out of the corridor and out into the open air, she was shocked by how nice the ship actually was. The only ship she had been on was the one carrying her to the island and that had been an adventure in itself. This ship, while it seemed to only be for cargo was a magnificent piece of wood and metal.

Most cargo ships she'd seen were all gray and uniform. His ship had character, as if the captain really put his heart and soul into the very floor of the vessel. If she hadn't already been drooling after the man, the Jolly Roger definitely would have sealed the deal for her.

A HALF HOUR later and she was back at her hotel room. Having checked in via her phone, she only needed to grab her key from the front desk and then she was slipping it into the lock and opening the door. The moment she stepped in, her heart stopped at the display around her room.

Sitting on every surface of the room was a dozen tiger lilies. So orange and vibrant in their color that just looking at them made her eyes hurt. Wendy hated flowers. They were a useless waste of money and made her nose itch.

Fighting off a sneeze, she went around to all the vases looking for a card. She finally found one hidden in the bedroom. They were from Peter. Of course.

*Meet me at the Hideaway Bar at noon.*
*Bring the evidence.*
*Miss you*
*Peter*

She frowned at the commanding tone of his words and the loving words added, as if an afterthought, before heading to take a shower. She needed to get the magic completely off her before she figured out how to get rid of the flowers and Peter Pan.

Getting under the hot spray, Wendy let her mind wander. She had barely been on the island for more than a day, and she had already been mind-fucked and kidnapped. It was making her long for the awkward office back in New York. At least there, she knew she wasn't getting screwed in any manner.

But there was something about the captain. James. The story he had told her about how the ship got its name, while he said it was a joke, she felt like maybe it wasn't. There was a kind of sadness to his eyes when he had retold the tale, as if it was more than just a mission gone badly. Like maybe he felt responsible.

Was that why Peter thought he was a criminal? Because he had caused his friend's death? If so, why did Peter even care? He was fae, not military.

Wendy pondered over these thoughts as she scrubbed her body. By the time she was done, her skin was red and she had probably scrubbed a layer off, but she was clean. Now to stay that way.

THE HIDEAWAY BAR was exactly like its namesake. It was a dark and small hole in the wall meant to discourage tourists. She would've been happy to find it had she not been there for a different reason.

She scanned the little room looking for Peter's red hair. Not seeing it, she approached the bar where Bear seemed to be tending.

"Well, look who it is. Miss too good for us," Bear leered at her. "Did you have a nice night with the croc?"

"Croc?" Wendy ignored his insult, cocking her head to the side.

"That blasted pirate you were supposed to be getting the goods on, not fucking," Bear growled leaning forward on the bar. "No wonder a girl like you would get caught in his jaws."

"A girl like me? I don't know what you mean. But I'm here to see Peter. Where is he?" She crossed her arms over her chest, her 'don't fuck with me' face in place.

"Exactly." He pointed out, though she had no idea what he meant. "Your boy is in the back. But I wouldn't go in there if I were you. He's busy."

Bear turned from her and went back to doing whatever the hell he had been doing before. The door he gestured to was next to the bar. Wendy contemplated waiting for Peter to come out. It was already passed noon. She had fought with herself for over an hour on whether or not she should go and ended up making herself late.

James had told her to stay away from Peter, but she couldn't let what he'd done to her go. He needed to know what he did was wrong, and that she was going to make him pay for it. Hopefully, she could keep her wits about her to say so.

Making sure her phone was on voice recording, she tucked it into the front of her jeans as she pushed the back door open. As she made her way into a hallway and then into a dimly lit room, Wendy began to get a creepy tingle under her skin.

It was bigger than the bar but the lighting was worse. Purposely done there were dark red lights lining the walls making the room seem seductive and dangerous. As she stepped into the area, she heard moans coming from the other side of the room.

Lying on a mattress placed on the floor was Peter, with only a pair of pants on. His head was thrown back and pleasure etched his face. His hand was buried in the hair of a dark haired girl who had her lips wrapped around his cock.

Gasping, Wendy turned on her heel and made for the door, but paused when Peter's voice called out.

"Wendy?" his voice was filled with need, and it made her insides clench even as her stomach rolled.

Even though they had been apart, he still had some kind of hold over her. James was right, she shouldn't have come.

"Wait! Don't go." The command in his voice wouldn't let her move her feet toward the door. She fought with herself for control over her body and almost cried when she couldn't make it move.

"Come here." Her body twisted around to face where Peter sat. His hands still gripping the woman's hair, not even concerned with her seeing him with another woman.

"No." She shook her head at him, but still her feet moved.

"You're late," he continued, not acknowledging her words. "Did you bring it?"

"No." Wendy dug her heels into the ground, her nails biting into her hands.

"No, what? You didn't bring it?" Peter finally tapped the woman on the head signaling her to stop. "What were you doing the whole time at the croc's ship if you didn't even get anything on him?" Peter stood from the bed, not bothering to tuck himself back in his pants as he approached her.

"No," she said again, forcing her foot to take a step back. "Stay away from me."

Frowning at her, Peter kept coming. "What it is, Wendy? Didn't you like my flowers?" he smiled at her, showing his white teeth in the dark. "They're tiger lilies. Lily said they are every girl's favorite." He glanced back at the woman on the bed.

"No, I didn't. I hate flowers, they make me sneeze," she snarled, latching on to the fact that he had sent her flowers named after another girl. "Which you would know had you asked."

This time, Peter stopped. The frown on his face deepened and confusion filled his eyes. "What's wrong with you?"

"I'm finally thinking for myself, and I won't be your little sex puppet anymore. Is she one of them?" Wendy gestured to the girl behind him. "Is she one of your victims? Because I will have you know, you messed with the wrong woman. I'm a lawyer. I will make sure you pay for what you tried to do to me, and what you have no doubt done to countless others."

"Now, hold on a moment." Peter held his hands up. "No one is any one's sex puppet. Not unless they want to be anyways." He chuckled at his own joke. "Besides, who is going to believe you? I mean, no one is going to believe that you didn't want me. I mean look at me."

Wendy felt disgusted as the fae crowed on and on. How long had this been going on? Her eyes latched onto the semi-nude woman on the bed who seemed perfectly content to wait for Peter to return whenever he wished.

"Also, I'm on the council for supernatural creatures. Do you really think any of them would believe I would break my own law?" Peter laughed, not even paying her any mind as she made her way to the door.

Grabbing her phone out of her pocket, she clicked the button to stop recording and turned to him once more. "Peter Pan."

"Huh?" He stopped laughing to look at her at the door.

"Go fuck yourself." With that, she spun on her heel and stomped out of the bar and into the fresh air.

No more.

Hand wrapped around her phone, a smile curled up her face. She might have come to the Never Isles to relax but now she was going to destroy him. He would curse the day he ever laid eyes on her when she was done with him. Wendy knew just the man to help her do it.

# CHAPTER 6
## *JAMES*

IN THE MILITARY, many habits had been instilled in James. Most of them, he had abandoned as soon as he was able. Shaving was one task he hadn't been able to leave behind.

Most men nowadays used an electric razor, but James had learned from his commanding officer that faster didn't mean better. So, even while under time crunches and threats of enemy fire, he had always made time for his old-fashioned straight razor and brush.

Sliding the sharp edge along the length of his neck, his dark eyes focused on the task at hand, careful not to nick himself. He'd been shaving since he was barely old enough to have facial hair, but even one small move could cause him to end up with another mouth where there shouldn't be one.

Mid-swipe, a knock pounded on the door causing James' arm to jerk and a red rivulet of blood to trail down his throat. Cursing, James grabbed a towel from his wash station and pressed it to his new cut before turning to the door.

"What?" He growled out, irritation littering his voice.

"Uh, Capt'n." Smith's hesitant voice called out through the door. "There's a Miss ... uh Wendy here to see you."

James' scowl turned into a smile at the prospect of seeing the lovely brunette.

When he had come to let the woman out of her chains the next morning, he hadn't been able to stop staring at her. Even in her sleep, she was the most beautiful thing he had ever seen. It was hard enough for him to let her go let alone keep his hands to himself. Now she was back and by her own choice, he hoped.

"Let her in." James turned back to the mirror, his eyes on the door as he resumed his daily routine.

He almost nicked himself again when his eyes landed on her. Dressed in a mid-thigh light blue sundress, she was quite a vision compared to the jeans and t-shirt he had first seen her in. His hand tightened on the handle of his razor. James struggled to keep his eyes on her face and not on the swell of her breasts as the fabric clung to her every movement.

Lucky for him, he wasn't the only one affected because when her eyes took in his shirtless form, a small gasp fell from her lips. James had to force himself not to laugh. Sliding the razor along his cheekbone, his eyes met hers through the mirror.

"You've come back, I see." He tried to keep the laughter out of his voice as she seemed to fight to find an appropriate place to look besides his bare skin. "Hopefully in your right mind this time?"

Clearing her throat, her eyes snapped up to his. "Yes. I'm fine now. That's what I wanted to speak to you about." She took a deep breath and stepped toward him, her skirt swishing around her thighs. "I wanted to thank you for what you did last night. I would have never known what was going on if you hadn't interfered."

"Nothing to thank me for. Anyone would have done the same." James shrugged and covered his face with the towel to wipe away the rest of the shaving cream.

"But that's the thing. I don't think they would." Wendy's hands wrung together and she pulled her lip in between her teeth. "From what I've seen, I don't think anyone I saw would have done anything as soon as they figured out I was under Peter's influence." She paused for a moment as if gathering her strength. "Does being on the Council for Supernatural Creatures really give you that much power? I mean, it was like they didn't care that what he was doing could be illegal."

"Being on the council is like being a celebrity to some of these people. To the fae it means that he isn't just popular. One wrong move and he can have them sent before the council, no matter if they were innocent or not," James explained, and then paused his eyes narrowing. "How did you even know he was on the council? It's not something he spreads around."

Wendy snorted. "It wasn't that hard to get him to tell me. He practically crowed about it for half an hour when he told me I couldn't do anything to him." She chuckled and then became serious. "But his being on the council does worry me, as I hope to get him on misuse of magic charges. That's why I came by actually." She stopped babbling long enough to look at James.

"You went to see him again, didn't you?" Her eyes widened as James stalked toward her. His face darkened and his gaze as sharp as the blade he had just had in his hand. "After I had warned you not to go, you went and did it anyway."

"I'm a grown woman. I can make my own decisions." Wendy crossed her arms over her chest, pressing her breasts up against the opening of her dress. "Besides, I knew what I was going into."

"Did you? Did you really?" The darkness in James' voice couldn't be contained as he stalked toward her.

"Of course, I did. I'm a lawyer, not an imbecile. I know how magic works. Once someone figures out they are under a spell it makes it harder for them to be tricked again." Wendy's voice broke as James cornered her against the small desk in his bedroom on the ship.

"Harder, yes. Impossible, no." James placed one hand on either side of her, thoroughly trapping her.

"W ... what are you doing?" Wendy visibly swallowed and licked her lips, drawing his dark eyes down to the movement of her tongue.

"I'm checking to see if you've been placed under his spell once more." His hand came up to cup her face, holding her in place as he surveyed her. "While having knowledge of the spell does weaken its effects, the chances of you being caught again are still high. Too high for you to go against him on your own. So tell me, do you still crave his touch?" James placed a muscular thigh between hers, pressing up against her heat. "Does the feel of my touch repulse you?"

"No." Her voice came out breathless. If he was hearing right a bit needy.

"Are you sure?" He rocked his thigh against her, the arm not holding her face up to his wrapped around her waist, bringing her closer still. Wendy moaned, her eyes closing to him. His question unanswered. "Answer me." His voice whispered in her ear but she only opened her mouth and gasped.

"Fine." James moved away from her, causing her eyes to snap open to look at him. Confusion and need splayed across her face and James was half tempted to continue, but he needed to be sure.

"Why did you stop?" The hurt and disappointment in her voice made James' heart clench, but he stilled his back for what he had to do next.

"If you want my help, I have to be one hundred percent sure you aren't under his influence anymore. We can't have you jumping sides mid-courtroom. Those books, for example, showed specific dates and times of where I will be and those could get me into trouble in the wrong hands," James explained keeping his distance from her, the next part was going to be hard enough to restrain himself.

"I'm not under anyone's influence, James. And I would never jeopardize a case for some guy," she snarled. But James just shook his head.

"That's not good enough. I need to know for sure."

Wendy frowned and placed her hands on her hips. "Fine. Then how do I prove I'm not under his influence?"

"Turn around." James kept his eyes on hers and not on the thighs that would soon be bare to him. The thought of the next test alone caused him to harden in his jeans.

"What? Why?"

"Just do it." His voice commanded and he said a silent prayer when she complied. "Hands on the desk. Lean forward. Farther."

With her bent over his desk, her shapely behind facing him James did everything in his power to keep from groaning. She had the most delectable backside and that was with clothes on!

"What am I doing, James?" Wendy asked him from her place on his desk. James didn't answer as he slid the back of her skirt up. "What? What the hell are you doing?" She tried to get up from the desk, but James placed a hand on her back, pressing her back down.

"Relax. This will be harder on me than you." He gave a dark chuckle. "You never know, you might enjoy it."

Struggling against his hold, Wendy's voice took on a panicked screech. "Let me up, I'm not having sex with you, not even to prove I'm not under a spell. I'll take down Peter on my own."

"One, I never said anything about sex, and if we were going to have sex, it wouldn't be on this crappy work desk. It'd break in an instant. Secondly." James flipped her skirt up over her waist baring her lacy white panties to his view. "… you can't get Pan without me and you know it. Now hold still."

Sliding a hand over her left cheek, he tried not to let out a noise at the feel of her flesh against his hand. It was wrong that someone so smart-mouthed had such a perfect ass. There had to be some law against it. Though, as she constantly reminded him, she was a lawyer. It was probably mandatory to have a fabulous ass.

After massaging for a moment, he swung his hand back and then with a loud smack, brought it back down on her skin. An alarmed sound came from her but she didn't fight him or protest. James wouldn't have heard anyway, since his attention was solely on the lovely shade of pink her cheek was turning.

Perfect. She was perfect. How was he going to get through this without trying to rut her like a dog?

His hand moved back over the pink flesh, caressing the sting away before he continued with the other side. His hand swung down creating a sound of flesh on flesh before he soothed the skin and started again.

Over and over again, he did it. Each time his caresses lasted just a bit longer and moved just a bit closer to the inside of her thighs. The sounds that came from Wendy only spurred him further. She might have protested at the beginning, but she was thoroughly enjoying herself now.

Enough so that James felt confident to ask, "Do you want Peter Pan?"

"No! God no, don't stop," Wendy moaned out when his hands paused on her waist.

Almost moaning, James told her, "You have to say the words." Before bringing his hands back down to her ass, this time rubbing his hardness against her.

"Say the words?" She couldn't seem to get her voice any more than James could keep his hands off her. James lifted her a bit so he could press himself against the crook of her thighs and she whimpered. "I don't want Peter Pan."

Grunting, James thrust against her. "Louder." Reaching around he pressed his fingers to the front of her panties to find her clit, twisting his fingers down on it through her drenched panties.

Wendy's voice came out a scream, "I don't want Peter Pan!"

"That's my girl." With one more swipe of his fingers, James forced himself to remove his hands and place her back on the ground. Taking a step back, James adjusted himself in his pants before turning away from her and back to his wash basin.

"What? That's it?" There was a strain on her voice and a bit of desperation that James couldn't help but smirk at.

"Yes, that's it. You've proved you're not under the influence of Peter Pan anymore." Glancing in the mirror, he pretended to check his face for any spots he missed shaving. But all the while watching the brunette as she gaped at him.

After a minute or so, she composed herself, but James could tell she was still miffed at him. Her nose was scrunched up and her hands were closed into tight fists. He would have been worried except they needed each other. If they were going to bring Peter Pan down they would both need to keep their heads and pants on.

"You can see yourself out I can assume?" James picked up his shaving brush, swishing it around in its container.

With a little stomp of her foot, Wendy sniffed and marched to the door. Swinging the door open, she barreled through it but not before calling out over her shoulder, "Fuck you, James Clocker."

# CHAPTER 7
## *WENDY*

WHEN SHE GOT back to her room, she tried to phone her friend Nana but she didn't pick up. She left a message asking her to find out everything she could about cases for misuse of magical powers. Wendy needed her to find out whatever she could about the magical influence laws and how she could prove it in court. As a professional, she was not one to rely purely on he-said-she-said.

The second thing she did was begin packing her suitcase. Since she hadn't unpacked her suitcase it made it all the easier to pack back up when she only had her dirty clothes and toiletries to throw back into it.

With her suitcase zipped up and ready to go, Wendy made her way to the door. Pausing in the doorway, she surveyed the lovely room she hadn't been able to fully enjoy, and all the complimentary amenities she would no doubt be missing out on.

But she couldn't stay here. Peter knew where she was and she couldn't take the chance that he'd come by to see her. James might have cleared her of magical influence, but that didn't mean she wanted to be anywhere near the fae if she could help it.

Where she was going to stay though was a problem. She'd stormed out of James' bedroom before they could really get to that part. Though, she was sure he would agree that she couldn't stay in the hotel anymore. Her lips quirked up at the thought of the face James would make when she showed back up on his ship, her suitcase in tow.

The thought of seeing him again made her face heat. She couldn't believe she'd let him manhandle her into his little test. Then there was the way she had reacted to his hands on her. She had no doubt that her bottom was still red from where he had smacked her, and she would be a liar if she didn't admit that she still throbbed from the lack of release.

Wendy wasn't a prude by any means and knew that some people liked that kind of pain with their sex, but she had never thought she would be one of them. The way that James had pressed his hardened length against her though showed he was enjoying their interaction more than just to make sure she was completely on his side. It made her hope that perhaps the situation would call for him to bend her over his desk again, but this time with an orgasm involved.

With a small laugh, she closed the door behind her and walked down the hallway, away from her unused room and into the elevator. As she waited for it to take her to the lobby her phone chirped at her, signaling an incoming call. Seeing who it was, a broad smile covered her face before she hit the accept button, putting the phone to her ear.

"Nana! I was beginning to think you forgot about me. What took you so long to call me back?" Wendy asked her longtime friend and ex-coworker.

"Me? You are the one who up and quit and then disappeared off the face of the earth. I'm doing everything I can to keep it together at the office now that you're gone." Her best friend's voice filled with mock despair.

Nana still worked at Darling and Darling, but swore every day she was going to leave because Wendy wasn't there anymore. Every time she had to talk Nana out of it. There was no reason for her to lose her career because the boss was a cheating bastard. But it was good to know that her friend had her back. She was going to need that loyalty now.

"I told you, Nana. I went to the Never Isles. Hold on a sec." Gathering her things from the elevator, she stepped out into the lobby. Parking her bag by the sitting area, she leaned against one of the tall pillars that decorated the reception area. "Okay, I'm back."

"So how is the fae world?" Wendy could hear the desperate curiosity in her friend's voice. Nana loved all things supernatural, especially the fae. She swore they had the most delicious men and would snag herself one someday, that was, if she ever got a day off.

"It's like I thought it would be, and not." The answer as evasive as possible.

"What do you mean?"

Wendy sighed. She knew that her friend was going to be able to tell something was wrong. It was hard to hide anything from someone she'd known since she was in nappies.

"It's very touristy," she explained. "And the fae well ..."

"Yes? Are they as scrumptious as I've heard? Tell me you took some photographs?" The eagerness in her friend's voice caused Wendy's heart to ache. She hated to be the bearer of bad news.

"No, I didn't take any pictures. And the fae ... yes, they are more attractive than the hot fudge on a double-decker chocolate cake."

"I knew it!" Nana jumped in before Wendy could finish explaining. "I knew there was a reason they were hole up on that island. They wanted to keep all their yummy goodness to themselves. It's selfish, I tell you. Pure selfishness."

Eyes rolling at the pout in her friend's voice, she glanced around the room for any eavesdroppers, before lowering her voice, "Nana, there's something else."

"More than the fae hotties? Please tell me you've hooked up with one already, you so need a good shag after the Michael debacle. Did you know that they transferred that little slut he was cheating on you with?" Her voice lowered as if she didn't want to be overheard.

"No!" Wendy let herself be distracted by the news of her rival's descent out of the Darlings' good graces.

"Yes!" Nana confirmed. "Just shortly after you quit, she made this huge scene, and I heard he told her she could either resign or be transferred to their office in Florida. Can you imagine? Going from New York to Florida! And she wouldn't even be working on big cases, their Florida office is used to give back to the supernatural community. Kind of an outreach program. So she won't even be a real lawyer anymore, just some nobody handling civil disputes." Nana snorted. "Serves her right if you ask me."

"That's not very nice, Nana. We don't even know the girl. She could be perfectly nice and just happen to get caught up in Michael's game, just like me. Anyways, no more getting off topic. I called because I needed you to—"

"Get everything I could on magical influence laws. Yeah, yeah. I got your message," Nana interrupted again. "I had one of the paralegals email it over to you, it should be in your inbox."

"Thanks, Nan. I'll check it out tonight." Wendy moved away from the pillar and stepped toward the exit. She walked out of the hotel and made her way to the docks. It was lucky the island was so small. The majority of its amenities were close together.

"What do you need it for anyways? Did something happen?" Nana's voice went from bossy to concern.

"Let's just say that I found out firsthand what the fae can do and it wasn't all rainbows and orgasms." Wendy let the distain drip from her words.

"Ah man, don't tell me that kind of shit. Now you've gone and burst all my perfectly good fantasies. What am I going to masturbate to now?"

Wendy couldn't help but laugh at her friend's disappointment, even though she knew she had no problem in that department.

"I'm sure you'll think of something."

After a moment or two, Nana quit bitching about Wendy ruining her life and got serious. "So, do you need back up or what? I can get a flight and be over there in no time."

Smiling down at the floor, her heart filled with love for Nana. She might be a bit self-absorbed but she had no problem dropping everything when she was in need.

"As much as I'd love to have you by my side, what about work?"

"Them? Fuck them. They already fucked my best friend. As far as I'm concerned, they are dead to me. More than dead. They are scum at the bottom of the ocean to me. They are lucky I haven't run their asses over." Wendy began to laugh so loudly that she was attracting the attention of those loitering in the lobby.

"Am I going to have to defend you in court? I mean I know you want to help my tanking career and all, but I don't think getting arrested for murder is the way to go."

"Darling, don't you know? I would do anything for you and that tight ass."

Snorting at her friend's declaration, Wendy cleared her throat. "Seriously, don't worry about me. This is small fish. Nothing I can't handle." Wendy was about to tell her goodbye when her eyes landed on the Jolly Roger.

"Well if there is anything you need, just to talk or help with whatever case you have brewing, let me know. I'm here for you." Nana's reassuring voice spurred on Wendy's curiosity.

"There is one thing." Pausing for a moment, she chewed on her bottom lip before blurting out. "Have you ever been spanked?"

# CHAPTER 8
## *JAMES*

AS SOON AS Wendy left his bedroom, James dropped the shaving brush and headed straight for the bathroom, where he proceeded to have a long cold shower.

That woman was going to be the death of him. There was no way they were going to be able to work together on getting Pan behind bars if James couldn't keep his hands, or his dick, to himself. He could see a lot of cold showers in his future and he wasn't happy about it.

The sweet relief his shower presented him hadn't lasted long. Too soon after, the cause of his torment was back on the deck of his ship with a suitcase in hand. His eyes watched her from his post above the crew as she took in her surroundings.

Her eyes were full of determination and caution. Good. She had finally learned to pay attention.

It would be sad if they went to all the trouble and work to get Pan arrested for her to get blindsided again by the fae. Just because Pan couldn't affect her didn't mean he couldn't get one of his lackeys to spell her instead. James would have to make sure she stayed clear of any and all supernatural creatures from now until the trial.

Smith walked up to her muttering something James couldn't make out. Wendy responded with a matter of fact look on her face and poor Smith seemed to be beside himself as he no doubt tried to persuade her from whatever it was she wanted. But the old man was no match for the big shot lawyer, and seemed to concede with a lowering of his head as he made his way toward James.

When her eyes finally fell on him, the delightful redness that spread across her face and down her neck, caused his cock to stiffen again. It was the exact shade her lovely ass had been when he had finished with her. All thoughts of keeping away from her flew from his mind when all he could think about was bending her over once more but this time, he wouldn't stop.

James groaned and tried to think of something other than what it would be like pounding into her soft flesh, and could have kissed Smith when he came up to him.

"Capt'n. That woman is back again." The very sight of the older man deflated any fluid in James' groin and he decided then that Smith must be in the room whenever he and Wendy met. Otherwise, nothing would ever get done.

"I see that, Smith," James growled. "But what is she doing here with her suitcase?"

"Um, she means to stay here, Capt'n," Smith stuttered, wringing his hand in front of him.

"Stay here!" James' eyes latched onto where Wendy stood with her arms crossed over her chest and her tiny foot tapping away on the hard floor of the deck. "We'll see about that." James pushed passed

Smith and made his way down the stairs, his eyes locked onto the brunette.

There was no way she was staying there. He wouldn't make it one day if he was constantly taking cold showers just to function right. James had to find a way to get her off his ship and out of his mind.

His lips crept up into what could be described as a wicked smile, causing Wendy to pause in her tapping and take a step back. This might be easier than he thought.

"What do you think you are doing?" James snarled, grabbing hold of her arm before she could back away further.

"Exactly what I planned to do before you assaulted me." Wendy snapped back, not trying to get away from him but leaning forward so her face was right up to his. "I can't be around Peter again, you said so yourself. Which means I can't stay at the hotel. The only logical choice is for me to stay with you."

James opened his mouth to interrupt but was cut off when she continued.

"Besides, it only makes sense for us to be together if we are going to have any chance of getting him locked up where he belongs."

He let her pull her arm from his grasp, her words making sense, though he wanted it not to be true. "Whether we like it or not, you need me as much as I need you."

"Fine, but there will be some ground rules," James snapped, trying not to stomp his foot like a petulant child.

"Of course. I wouldn't expect anything else." The smile she gave him could only be classified as sweet and innocent, though he knew underneath it, she was probably congratulating herself for winning.

"Smith!" James turned back to where Smith was watching, a petrified look on his face and waved him over. "Smith will take your bag to one of the rooms on board. We don't have much. This isn't a luxury cruise ship, so don't get your hopes up."

"I like your ship, but not so much its captain." The tone of her voice made him want to turn her over his knee and give her the spanking she and he both wanted but he kept his hands to himself. The fact that she liked his ship alone was making it hard enough to behave; if she kept mouthing off he didn't know what he would do.

A day, that's all he gave himself before he gave into temptation. With her smart mouth and her delicious rump, it would be a miracle if he lasted that long.

"Take our guest's bag to one of the rooms I reserve for crew members," James ordered, letting Smith pick up her suitcase as he turned back to a frowning Wendy. "Most of the crew members have homes here, or on the mainland, so rarely do they sleep on deck. You should be safe there."

"And what about you?" She followed him as he made his way back to his place on top of the overseer's platform.

"What about me?" James went back to work on the ledgers he had been working on before she had shown up.

"Do you have a home or do you live on the ship?" Wendy leaned against the side of his desk, making it impossible for him to ignore her.

"For the time being, I live here." His eyes reread the calculations he had started, but he couldn't get his head to focus on them with her this close to him. "Now, about those ground rules."

"Yes." Jumping in, she pressed herself closer to him so she was in his line of sight. "First rule, look at me when I'm talking to you. It's rude."

Snapping his head up from the book, his face ended up a hairs breath away from hers, causing a smirk to form as she blushed.

"Fine. Rule two." He brought himself into her personal space, trapping her between the table and his body. "No smart mouthing. I know that might be difficult for you and all, but this is my ship and I will run it how I see fit. If you have an opinion, keep it to yourself."

Brown eyes narrowed at him and her lips pursed together she said, "All right. Then you have to keep your hands to yourself. No trying to sneak into my room looking for someone to stroke your ego."

James gave a dark chuckle, moving in close when she shivered. "Honey, if I needed someone to stroke my ego, I wouldn't need to ask for it. You were plenty ready to give it to me right there on the table." His leg shifted until it was between her thighs, putting them in a similar position as before.

Her breath caught in her throat and he watched as a display of emotion ran across her face. She seemed to be fighting with herself as much as he was to keep her desires in check. James knew he was in for a ride when the emotion she decided on was defiance.

"I'm not the one who started dry humping me when he was supposed to be testing my validity." The curve of her breast pushed into him as she inched closer to him. "If anyone will be begging for it, it will be you, Captain."

The sound of his title falling from her lips was the last straw and James' lips found themselves pressed against hers, a groan ripping from his throat.

He hadn't even made it a day.

# CHAPTER 9
## *WENDY*

A STARTLED GASP fell from her mouth as his lips crashed onto hers. As if he was waiting for it, his tongue swept in, overtaking her mouth like he owned it. Not caring that they were out in the open and his crew was probably getting a show, Wendy kissed him back, her hands finding their way into his hair.

Tugging him closer to her still, she wrapped her leg around his hips grinding herself down onto the thigh between her legs. Wendy could feel his hardened length pressed against her stomach, and a desperate needy sound came from her throat. She hadn't been able to tell when he had her bent over his desk, but like this, she could feel every glorious inch of him. It made her ache to have him inside her and she couldn't wait to find out if he really was a big as he felt.

Dragging her mouth away from him long enough to take a breath, she opened her eyes briefly and paused when she caught sight of the gaping sailors.

Blushing down to her toes, she ducked her head down.

"What is it?" James asked when she wouldn't look up at him so he could capture her lips once more.

"We have company," she muttered, her face inflamed.

His body angled away from her to look behind him, and he cursed, "What the hell are you looking at? This ain't no peep show. Get back to work!"

When the men dispersed, Wendy finally glanced up from the hole she had pretended to crawl in. She couldn't believe she had let him kiss her like that in front of everyone. They were practically dry humping. Sure, she had egged him on, hoping for that exact reaction, but she hadn't thought he would do it right there!

"Sorry about that, sweetheart." James brushed a hair behind her ear and then cupped her face so she was looking up at him. "Bunch of perverts, the lot of them." He gave her a cheeky grin that she couldn't help but return.

"It's all right. We kind of got carried away." Pulling her bottom lip in between her teeth to chew on it, she disentangled herself from his grasp. "I'm just going to ... uh ... go to my room. It's this way, right?" She pointed a thumb behind her toward the stairs.

"Let me walk you." James offered, his long legs taking no time to jump in front of her to lead the way.

Wendy kept her eyes down as they walked passed the crew. Thankfully, they had the decency not to laugh and jeer, though there were some whispers. She followed behind James as he led her into the corridor she had exited just that morning. Instead of turning toward his room, he went the opposite way where a long row of doors stood.

Stopping in front of one that was already opened, where the man Smith had sat her bag so she could find it, James gestured her inside.

The room was small and sparsely furnished with a single bed and a dresser. There was a tiny closet, big enough to hang a coat or two inside but that was pushing it. There was one thing that was glaringly missing and it just wouldn't do.

"Where's the bathroom?"

Clearing his throat, James rubbed the back of his head an embarrassed look on his face. "The crew uses a communal bathroom." When Wendy's jaw dropped, he quickly added, "but you are free to use mine whenever you want. I wouldn't want the crew to get distracted by the luscious body you have under that tiny dress of yours."

Nodding her head, she blushed at the heat in his eyes as he scanned up and down her dress. It was like he could see straight through her dress and to her bare skin beneath. She shivered at his gaze, her core throbbing in need. It made her wonder when he would kiss her again.

Before she could ask, James was next to her cupping her face in his hands. "Rule three," he said before pressing his lips to hers in an overwhelming but chastise kiss. "We have to do that again." He smirked before closing the door on her shocked expression.

AFTER JAMES LEFT, Wendy collapsed on the bed. The last twenty-four hours had been exhausting, exhilarating, and at times downright frustrating. All she wanted was to have a large glass of wine and a hot bubble bath. But that required using the dark haired captain's bathroom, where he could walk in on her at any point in time. Maybe even join her? Her insides clenched with need at the thought.

She had never met someone as intense as James Clocker. With just one look, he had her weak in the knees and her panties drenched. Not even Michael had made her feel that way. The captain only had to glance her way and she was ready to bend to his will, no magic spell required.

It wasn't like she hadn't been with anyone in a while. She and Michael had only broken up a few weeks ago. She'd like to think she hadn't reached the level of desperation that would have her running after any semi-attractive man with a decent dick between his legs. Though, remembering what the captain had sporting between his thighs made her face hot and her hand itch to continue where they had left off.

In her opinion, that was as good of a reason as any. If Nana had been there, she no doubt would have asked her what the hell was she waiting for. While she had no problem being the first one to make a move, and there was a certain chemistry between the two, there were more important things to worry about right now.

Peter Pan had to be stopped and since she couldn't bring herself to hunt down the delectable captain to finish what they started, Wendy needed to get some work done.

Pulling her laptop from her suitcase, she was lucky that the Pier Wi-Fi was close enough for her to check her email. Opening up her web browser, she logged into her email account to find the files that Nana's paralegal had sent her. Smiling, she clicked on the first file.

It described an instance where a human girl had been ensnared by a fae's magic which resulted in the current laws upheld by the council. The Council of Supernatural Creatures was mostly made up of fae. Though there were a few vampires and werewolves in the mix, the fae held the majority, probably because they came out first.

Most believed that the first supernaturals to come out of the closet were the vampires and werewolves when in fact it had been the fae.

Almost a decade ago, there had been a sudden outpouring of fae from portals all over the world, starting in a small town in Iowa. The news said that they were running from a bunch of fae gone bad but never really said what happened or why they decided to stay in the human world.

Though, once the supernatural cat was out of the bag, it was decided that a council of sorts needed to be formed to police the supernaturals. Since the humans were inept to deal with an irate troll or a faerie infestation, it was better off letting them deal with their own kind, though that didn't always work out in the favor of humans.

The girl, who had been bespelled, had barely been eighteen and was from the area where the first outbreak had occurred. It was discovered that the fae who imprisoned her, had kept her as his unwilling sex slave for months, not that she knew about it while under his control. During that time, her family had filed a missing person's report, desperate to find their missing daughter.

The Council of Supernatural Creatures had been alerted, but since there had been no proof that the girl had been taken by one of them, they weren't going to stick their noses in it. The police eventually found the girl at the fae's residences, completely and utterly under his spell. They had to drag her away in restraints just to get her to leave the house. From the reports, it looked like she went under intensive hypnotherapy to free her of his hold, and they still had doubt on whether or not she would ever be truly free.

Wendy shivered. That could have been her. It had almost been her. If it hadn't been for James, she might never have gotten out from under Peter's spell. It made the case much more important. She couldn't let that happen to another girl, especially not by Peter Pan, a member of the very council that was supposed to uphold those laws.

The thought of the fae made her see red. Wendy hated to see those in charge abuse their power, using it to prey on the weak and defenseless. The fact that she had been so easily bespelled hurt her pride and she wanted nothing more than to show she wasn't some pathetic woman that needed saving. The only way she could fight him was through the law, and that was something she knew well.

Going back to her computer screen, she scanned until she got to the part about what happened to the fae in question. How did they deal with supernatural criminals? They couldn't put them in a human prison, there was no way the humans would survive, and she doubted it would keep them there for very long. Some of the supernaturals were strong, so strong that they could smash through walls and bend metal to their will. Others, like faeries, were so small they could fly right through the bars of the cell.

The fae that had taken the girl had indeed been caught, but not until months later when he tried to kidnap another girl. His name was Bastian and from the reports, once they knew a fae was involved, the council had sent their Moderator to hunt him down. A woman she had only seen once in passing on the television, with almost white hair and striking blue eyes. Wendy had always wanted to meet the woman who was the enforcer of the supernatural laws, but had never had the pleasure.

Glancing back at the report, it said the fae in question had a history of misuse and would be properly punished, but the elusive council gave no other explanation than that. With an aggravated sigh, Wendy kept going through the files, each one not much more helpful than the first. It seemed like the council dealt with the problems on their own, with little to no description of what happened to the supernaturals or their punishments.

Giving up on finding out anything that would appease her, Wendy poured over the other reports, looking for any sort of clue that might help her with her case. What kind of evidence did they need? Would her word be good enough? She doubted it. Unless she had someone who knew from prior incidents, or someone currently bespelled, there was no way to prove that Peter had done anything to her.

A knock on her door pulled her from the computer screen and before she could tell them to come in the door cracked open, revealing a curious James.

"Are you going to stay in here all night?" His eyes landed on her computer and then back to her. "Did you find anything?"

Wendy looked at the time. It had been hours since she had first sat down to look over the files and her stomach told her it was near dinner time.

Closing her laptop, she stood from the bed. "No, unfortunately not yet. There are a few precedents that have potential but really, right now it comes down to proof. I mean I have this." She picked her phone up and played the recording she had of Peter for him. "But he doesn't directly say he was using magic on women and he even denies it."

"You can't use it against him at all? He blatantly bragged that he couldn't get in trouble even if he had done something. That has to mean something, doesn't it?" James' brows furrowed his face full of the same frustration she felt.

"To a judge and jury? No." Shaking her head she continued. "While it is suspicious and might make them keep an eye on him, it won't get him convicted of anything." Wendy sighed and ran a hand through her hair. "What we need is cold hard evidence, and unfortunately there is no physical proof that he used magic on me." Wendy held her hands out as if to show him there was nothing there.

James' eyes slid down her form, the frustration on his face morphing into a dark heat. Taking a step forward, his voice was low and husky, "I don't know. I can't really tell with all those clothes on. Maybe I should take a closer look?"

Laughing nervously, Wendy let herself be cornered in the small room. When he placed his hands on either side of her and she breathed in his scent. A deep yearning filled her. Wendy angled her head up, offering her lips to him but before he could take them a throat cleared behind them.

"Uh … Capt'n? Dinner is ready."

# CHAPTER 10
## *JAMES*

FUCKING SMITH. JUST when James was about to taste her succulent lips his first mate comes to cock-block him. He would fire Smith if he thought the nervous little man was even capable of doing it on purpose.

"We'll be there in a second," he snarled his eyes still focused on Wendy's lips, which had turned down in a frown at his words.

"Actually, we are coming right now." She pushed passed him, giving him a what-the-hell-is-wrong-with-you look, before smiling sweetly at Smith. "Could you show me the way, please? James, are you coming?" she asked over her shoulder.

"In a minute," he growled, ducking his head down in frustration. He took a deep breath to calm his raging erection. Think of anything. Faeries. Pan's smug face. The last one did the trick, and his cock deflated like a balloon.

Rubbing a hand over his face, he shook his head and chuckled. That woman was going to be the death of him. One minute she was a teasing little minx, and the next a fiery vixen demanding he do her bidding. Which James seemed only too happy to oblige.

What was she doing to him? He was the one usually in charge in, and out, of the bedroom. Giving up control wasn't a luxury he could afford, and he didn't think he would be able to have it anytime soon. With Wendy, though, the rules went out the window and all he could think of was sinking into her hot, wet folds.

And there he went again. It was impossible for him not to be constantly turned on when it came to her. He couldn't wait to get her into his bedroom and under his command. Then they would see who was following whose orders.

Laughing to himself, James opened the door to his office where Smith had set up a table for two. Wendy was already seated and working on a glass of wine, he'd had the forethought to have Smith fetch a few hours ago. It was a good idea seeing how she was drinking it down like she had just come out of the Sahara Desert. Though, he couldn't imagine anyone going there now that it was overrun with dragon shifters.

"What took you so long?" Wendy placed her wine glass on the table, cocking her head to the side with a frown.

James' eyes went to Smith and then back to Wendy. "Uh, I had to take a call." He dropped into his chair, hoping to hide any leftover reaction to his previous thoughts and picked up his own glass.

"Uh-huh." Amusement twinkled in her eyes. "If that is what they are calling it these days."

Ignoring her smart mouth, James focused on the food on the table. He had Smith get their dinner from the island instead of the usual crap from the cook. They each had on their plate a serving of chips and generous size snapper fish. He could just imagine the expression on her face if she had seen, let alone, tasted what his so-called cook considered fine cuisine.

"Thank you, Smith. This looks great," James said, dismissing his first mate to find his own meal.

James began to work on his fish but stopped when he found Wendy watching him over her wine glass. "What?"

"Do you always dine separately from the crew, or is it just because of me?" Her lips were pursed together like she found displeasure in him dismissing Smith. It didn't seem that he could do much right in her presence.

"No, usually I eat while I work," James explained in between bites.

It took all that he had not to moan at the exquisite flavor filling his mouth. He hadn't had food from the island in a long time, too afraid that the locals would poison him on Pan's behalf. But now James would have to take that risk more often, the food was just too good to go back to the cook's old slop.

"So you're a workaholic?" Wendy asked, digging into her own snapper. Unlike him, she did not fight her reaction when she finally tasted her meal.

Head thrown back and eyes closed, the sound that came out of her throat was similar to that of when she had been underneath him. James almost threw her down on the table right then and there, dinner be damned.

"Good?" James' voice was throaty and filled with desire. His self-control was being whittled away with each moment he was in the same room as her. It was getting to be rather pathetic.

"Yes, quite." She opened her eyes and licked her lips. He resisted a groan of his own.

James imagined that very tongue sliding up and down his cock. The noises she would make would be the same as the ones she was making now. The vibrations would filter into him, causing him to cum right then and there, and like the naughty vixen she was, she'd swallow him down, licking her lips with a satisfied smirk, when she was finished.

Grabbing his glass, he downed half of it, thinking he was just torturing himself. He didn't know if she actually wanted to have sex with him. Sure, she had let him kiss her and grind against her ass but that didn't mean she was up for going the whole way. Though, if she didn't want it, she was giving one hell of a mixed signal.

"So," she started, pulling James' attention back to her, "I was thinking that since we don't have any physical evidence, it would be good to have you testify about Peter's past misdeeds. You know, anytime that you thought someone was under his spell, or anything really you could think of that could help our cause. What do you think?"

"No, absolutely not," James plainly stated, knowing that his words would cause an onslaught of questions and accusations. He wasn't wrong when her face scrunched up in confusion, and anger tinged her words.

"What? Why not? If we don't find some kind of proof we really just have my word against his, and I'm not walking into a courtroom without anything to back me up. The judge would take one look at me and laugh." Her eyes filled with unshed tears and his heart clenched. "I need you, James."

Oh if only those words were coming from her for a different reason, preferably while he was sunk deep inside her. Right now, they just made him depressed.

James sighed, as much as he wanted to help her and to have Pan locked up where he belonged, there was no way he was going to court to testify. He might as well rent a flashing sign telling the Navy exactly where to find him. No, he couldn't do it. He would just have to find another way to help her.

"I'm sorry, I just can't. I'm sure there is another way to get your case through." James stood firm on his decision even when her blue eyes went hard as ice.

"Fine." She wiped her mouth and stood from her seat. "If you aren't going to help me, there really is no reason for me to be on this ship after all. Thank you for the meal and for saving me before. I hope you have a good life hiding behind these walls you have built around yourself, you coward."

James jumped up from his seat as she made for the exit. His hand slammed down on the door just as she opened it, trapping her between him and the wood. Not giving her the chance to turn around, he pressed against her, letting her feel the full strength of him against her back.

"Don't assume you know me. You don't know what I've been through, why I'm here." His voice rumbled in her ear, and he almost laughed at the shiver that went through her.

"Then tell me," she countered. "Maybe I could help you in return."

She tried to push him away with her hands but James captured them in his own, pulling them up above her head. With her hands trapped she pressed back against him, her butt rubbing along the front of his pants.

Whether her actions were on purpose or not, James' cock hardened against her softness. His hips moved on their own as they glided his length up and down the crease of her ass, an appreciative sound coming from both of them.

"You wouldn't understand." He tried to reason as he placed open mouth kisses along her neck. "I'm not a good man. There are people looking for me."

A gasp ripped from her throat when he bit down on the junction between her neck and shoulder. "Then what Peter said was true, you are a criminal."

"Yes," James hissed as he used one hand to hold both of her wrists while he used the other to slide her dress up her legs until it was around her waist. "Does that bother you?"

Just as she said, "it should." His hand slipped between her thighs cupping her heat causing her words to turn into a whimper.

"But it doesn't?" he asked his fingers finding their way beneath the thin fabric of her panties, and he ground himself harder against her when he felt how wet she was. "You're so ready for me. Does being with a criminal turn you on? Is that why you became a lawyer? To get your rocks off?"

"No," she snapped and tried to pull her wrists from his grasp, her irritation at his accusation clear. "Let me go."

"I don't think you want me to." James flicked her clit and smiled against her neck as she cried out. "I think you secretly love this, being held down, helpless to my desires." He swirled his finger against her before sliding one finger inside her where she clenched around it. "I could do anything I wanted to you like this and you would just let me." Finger pumping in and out of her, she wiggled and gasped, each movement and sound causing his own need to build.

"No, that's not true," she gasped in protest, but her hips rocked against his hand, contradicting her words.

"I bet a part of you even loved it when you were bespelled. Got you out of your own head for once because what a woman like you really needs is a good, hard fuck." He drilled in his words with each thrust of his finger.

He didn't notice when she stiffened against him. He was just about to pull her panties down to bury himself inside her when she began to struggle against him.

"Get the fuck off me, you asshole," she screeched, bucking violently against him.

Confused at the sudden change in her demeanor, he immediately let go of her and took a step back. "What's wrong?"

Wendy spun around and her hand connected with his face. James' head snapped to the side, a burning pain starting in his cheek.

Angry and confused, James grabbed her hand before she could slap him again. "Woman, calm down. What is your problem?"

"Let me go, you pig!" She pulled on her arm, her face becoming flush. It spread across her cheeks and down into her dress, where his eyes lingered on her heavy chest. He was ashamed to admit part of him found her even more attractive yelling at him.

"Not if you are going to hit me again." He held his arm up as she tried to whack him with her other hand.

"You deserve it!" Snarling at him, she tried to kick him in the shins.

Wincing at the dull pain of her tiny feet hitting him, he finally let go. "What the fuck is your problem?"

"You!" She jerked away from him the moment he let her go. "How can you joke about being bespelled when you don't know what it was like? It's not sexy or funny. I might be tightly wound at times, but that doesn't mean I want to be mind-raped."

Finally realizing his mistake, James held his hands up. "All right, I'm sorry. I shouldn't have suggested you liked it. I didn't mean it that way at all." Taking a cautious step toward her, he placed his hands on her arms. "Honestly, I was caught up in the moment and wasn't thinking."

Frowning at him but not pushing him away, Wendy let him draw her into his arms. "Damn right you weren't," she muttered into his chest.

"I won't do it again, I promise." James stroked his hand down her hair, trying to soothe the upset woman. Frowning at his own stupidity, he didn't see fit to let her know that he did indeed know what it was like to be under their spell. Now wasn't the time.

When she calmed down after a few moments, James leaned back. "Why don't you go take a bath? I have some work to do and I'll just wait here. When you are done we can talk about the case some more, all right?"

"Okay." Her voice was small and uncertain. Inside he was dying to kiss away those emotions, but didn't think she would let him at this point.

"Do you remember where my bedroom is?" He opened the office door for her as she nodded her head. "All right, then I'll see you in a little while. Take your time, if you need anything just let me know."

The door firmly shut behind her, James collapsed against the wood. What the hell was going on with him? Why did he even think that was okay for him to say? He hadn't meant what he said.

At the time, all he could think of was how much she had teased him and how much he wanted to punish her for making him feel like a teenager. His dick had been the one talking, that was certain. Now he would be lucky if he got a chance to be with her, let alone get her to let him truss her up.

He had a shit storm to clean up that was for                                        sure.

# CHAPTER 11
## *WENDY*

SINKING INTO THE hot water, Wendy couldn't help the slight moan that escaped her lips. It felt so good to finally relax and let the water just melt all her cares away.

After she left James' office, she had moved as fast as her feet could carry her to the bathroom. Things had gotten a little too intense and with James' admission to Peter's accusations, Wendy was more than a little apprehensive about letting the captain into her pants.

She knew he had been hiding something, Wendy had guessed as much the first time she was here when he talked about his friend Rogers. But the way he was bouncing around, not giving her any real information, just teasing her with the fact that he was a bad guy, was really starting to bug her.

Peter said he was a criminal, and James just admitted that people were looking for him. The real question, though, was for what? Wendy didn't have some kind of thing for bad boys, it certainly wasn't the reason she became a lawyer. She couldn't help but feel that she wasn't wrong about James. He wasn't a bad guy, just misunderstood. If he was in trouble it had to be for a good reason, right?

Her fingers found their way to her neck where she could still feel where he bit down. There was a slight indent where his teeth had pressed into her skin. The thought of the electricity between them caused a liquid pleasure to run through her. There was so much heat between them it was almost unreal. Every time he touched her she found herself craving him more and more.

Hand sliding under the water, her fingers danced over her clit, and then traced her opening where she still throbbed from his touch. Coming to the Never Isles was supposed to be about getting away from the real world and having a little fun. While James could definitely give her what she needed in that department, was it what she desired?

More and more she found herself drawn to this man that was clouded by a shroud of mystery and danger. While she did require him for her case, she found herself craving to know more about him. Why was he in the Never Isles? Why did he live on his ship? And more than anything she wanted to know what it would be like to give into him.

Slipping out of the water, she wrapped a towel around herself. After using another towel to dry off her hair, she reached for her clothes only to turn up empty handed. In her rush to get away from James, she had forgotten to get clean clothes. Her eyes looked down at the discarded dress and thought about putting them back on for a moment but the idea disgusted her too much to bear.

Chewing on her lip, she contemplated whether or not she could get to her room without any of the men, let alone James, seeing her. He couldn't keep his hands off her fully dressed, there was no telling what he would do with her only in a skimpy towel.

She cracked the bathroom door open and peeked out into the bedroom. There was no sight of the captain or anyone else, so Wendy slipped out of the bathroom and sprinted across the room to the door. Taking a deep breath in, she opened the bedroom door and stuck her still-damp head out into the hallway. Once again, there was no one in sight. She dashed for her bedroom door and almost collapsed to the floor when she made it without anyone seeing her.

Making sure the rest of her was dry, Wendy dug through her suitcase to find something appropriate to wear for a meeting of the minds. It would probably be a good idea not to wear anything that could tempt them into another display like in his office. At least not until she found out what he did to get on the wrong side of the law.

Decision made, she dressed in a pair of lounge pants and a loose fitting t-shirt. She pulled her hair up into a messy bun and slipped her feet into a pair of flip flops. Walking down the hallway to James' office, she knocked on the door before opening it to find an empty room.

Confusion filled her and then panic. She had left her clothes in his bathroom! Spinning on her heel, she beelined it back to his bedroom. Without knocking, she threw open his door and came face to face with a very surprised, very *nude* captain.

Gaping at the sight of him, her eyes roamed up his long muscular legs, to his toned and supple butt that instantly made her want to grab a handful. He had broad shoulders that rippled with an underlying strength that only came from constant physical activity.

When he saw her standing in the doorway, he turned toward her slightly giving her a generous view of his front. If his butt hadn't been enough to make her drool, the sight of his cock before her about did her in. At her lingering gaze, it grew long and thick, answering her question if he really was as big as he felt.

Licking her lips, she forced her eyes from his crotch and to his face that was filled with so much want that her insides clenched involuntarily.

"I ... I forgot my clothes," she stuttered and blushed, her eyes looking anywhere but at the protruding member pointed in her direction.

"Oh, by all means." James gestured toward the bathroom. His voice was rough and held just a bit of humor.

Straightening her shoulders, she marched to the bathroom, not once looking at his naked form. Laugh at her would he? She would give him something to laugh about.

Grabbing her clothes off the bathroom floor, she stomped out of the room to find him waiting for her by the door. Stumbling for a moment, her hand reached out to touch his bare chest. Jerking back as if burned, her face heated even more before she pushed passed him, making sure to 'accidently' drop her panties on the ground.

"Wendy." This time there was no laughter in his voice. It sounded strained as if it was taking everything in him to stay where he was. "You forgot something."

Turning around to see James with her dirty panties clasped in his hand like it was his favorite toy, she smirked. "No, I didn't."

Then closed the door behind her with a snap.

SITTING IN HIS office was torture. Why had she done that? What was she thinking giving him her panties? Wendy thought she had decided to back off with the physical stuff not do more!

She could only blame it on her damn pride. The way he laughed at her when he found her gaping at his deliciousness, she just couldn't help herself. Now she was regretting ever going back for her clothes, tight ass or not.

Her mind wandered back to his face when she had left him, he had been shocked, of course, but something in his eyes was so feral, she knew she would pay for teasing him so. It made her wonder what he had done when she left.

Did he toss them in the trash or maybe he pressed them to his nose, inhaling her scent. She had to admit the thought of it made her ache with need.

Shaking her head, Wendy tried to focus on the case and not the distracting captain. Waiting for him to come back and to put her out of her misery was driving her wild. The inpatient half of her was begging her to go see what was taking so long, but the horny part of her was just looking for an excuse to see him naked again.

Luckily, before she could convince herself one way or the other, the office door opened and James stepped in. He was fully clothed, seeming to have taken a cue from her by wearing a t-shirt and pajama pants. His hair was still wet from his bath, causing some of his shirt to stick to him where the water had slid down into it.

Wendy licked her lips but stopped when James' eyes zeroed in on the movement. Stop antagonizing him, Wendy. Business first. He might be a serial killer, remember? That thought firmly put her libido in check but just barely. If he had come in without a shirt on, all bets would have been off — as well as her pants.

Hands in his pockets, James strode over to his desk and took a seat, a small smirk playing on his lips. "So, where should we get started?"

Wanting to knock the grin off of his face, Wendy went right for the balls. "How about we start with why you're a wanted man? Then we can decide if you being part of this case is really beneficial for either one of us?"

His dark eyes narrowed on her, the intensity in his gaze hitting her at the core. That man would have made one hell of a lawyer. She couldn't see any jury being able to say no to him, Wendy was having a hard time herself.

Sitting up straight, she struggled not to let him see her squirm. "Well?"

"It's not really a story I tell just anyone." The curtness in his voice made her resolve waver just a bit, but she locked her eyes with his anyways.

"It's a good thing I'm a lawyer then, isn't it? I'm not just anyone, and I need to know, not just for my safety but because of the case. Just like you don't want me jumping sides in the middle of the courtroom, I have to be sure that you won't get arrested the moment you step foot on the mainland."

When he still didn't budge, she sighed. "Come on, it can't be that bad, can it?"

"You'd be surprised." The hardness of his voice softened a bit and his eyes filled with an unnamed emotion that tugged on her heart.

Wendy waited for him to continue and almost opened her mouth to prod at him again when he spoke in a low, but haunted, tone.

"I joined the Navy when I was fresh out of high school," he started, his eyes firmly on something unseen. "I was never one for school, so college wasn't really an option. The first few years were easy, well, once you got passed basic training and being the newbie and all." James chuckled to himself at some kind of inside joke.

"You have to understand; unlike what some people say, being in the Navy is hard. Long hours in the middle of nowhere, with no way to just pop back home. It can press on anyone's sanity. I guess it's that way for most people who serve our country." He mused to himself before continuing, "So when I got offered a position to explore the new fae territory, it wasn't a surprise to anyone that I jumped at the offer. Plenty of others did too. They were tired of staring at the ocean. We wanted to see land, and we didn't care how."

He paused for a moment, and she leaned forward on the edge of her seat not wanting to miss a thing. It was so fascinating to hear what it was like in the military. Never being one for joining up herself, she could understand how it would be difficult being at sea for so long. The trip over from the mainland had been hard enough on her. She couldn't imagine doing it every day, all day. She drew her thoughts back to James when he started talking again.

"The Never Isles, such a stupid name, there's not even multiple islands it's only the one. Of course, Pan came up with it, so I shouldn't be surprised." James snorted getting off topic for a moment.

"I had wondered," Wendy politely mused, but she really wanted him to get back to the story.

"See, what people don't know about the Island is that it isn't really in the human world at all." His large hand stroked his jaw and he leaned back in his chair. "When you got here you felt it, right? Just as when the island comes within eye distance there is a floating feeling?"

She nodded, knowing exactly what he was talking about. They had warned them in orientation, before she ever got on the boat to come to the Island that they would have a brief floating sensation but not to be alarmed. It was just a barrier keeping out those who would seek to harm the fae on the Island. It had all seemed a little bit suspicious to her.

"Well, that floating feeling isn't a protection barrier." His eyes narrowed in on her. "It's a portal."

"A portal?" Her mouth dropped open in surprise. "But that's illegal. They can't just transport you somewhere without telling you. It's kidnapping."

"Of course they can." James chuckled. "You signed a waiver before you got on the ship, didn't you?" Wendy nodded solemnly. "Well, in that waiver, you are giving them permission to bring you over from the human world to the fae world. Though, they don't say it in those specific words."

The words in the waiver had been pretty subjective, and she would admit, she didn't pay as much attention to what was in it as she usually did. With having just broken up with Michael, she just wanted to be out of there as fast as possible. Now she was kicking herself for being so reckless.

"So, we are in the fae realm right now?" Wendy stood from her seat and looked out the window. "But it doesn't look like anything but the middle of the ocean." Her eyes scanned the darkened sea, searching for anything that would give away that they weren't in the middle of the Bermuda Triangle.

"Fae are tricky like that." Wendy jumped when James' voice sounded by her ear, and she spun around to find him inches from her. "The portal is new. Usually, they have to go through a hole they've created, but it takes a good amount of magic and a lot of upkeep to leave it open. The portal like the one around the Island is different."

"How?" She cocked her head to the side focusing on his face and not the fact that they were so close together again. "I mean, how are they different?"

He tucked a stray hair behind her ear, the brush of his fingertips burned her skin where they touched. "Instead of creating a hole, they found a way to make the space between the two worlds thinner by taking advantage of areas that have a higher concentration of magic."

"Like the Bermuda Triangle," she muttered, his presence so close to her beginning to affect her train of thought.

"Like the Bermuda Triangle," James agreed. He slid a hand down and around her waist, pulling her to him. Her body pressed against the length of his and she could feel where his train of thought was going by the stiffness against her stomach, causing butterflies to dance in her belly.

"So what happened when you got here?" She tried to get them back on topic, and the racing of her heart under control.

James' eyes darkened as he gazed down at her, as if it wasn't really her he was seeing, but someone else. She was no longer worried about his hands on her, but more worried about the words coming from his mouth.

"The world knew that the fae had a certain amount of influence over humans, we had been trained for it, but none of us really *knew* how much they could actually take over our minds. Or our bodies. Fuck, if only we'd known." A display of emotion overran him, so much so that Wendy placed her hands on the side of his face just to make him really see her.

"James, tell me, what happened?" Her voice quaked at the words that she was sure to come out of his mouth.

"They all died."

# CHAPTER 12
## *JAMES*

THE EMOTIONS THAT spread over Wendy's lovely face was not that of shock or horror, not like he had expected. Instead, her eyes were sad and filled with understanding, as if she knew what he was going to say, even though James hadn't confessed to it yet.

James hadn't talked about it with anyone before. Smith didn't even know the full extent of what he was actually running from, but James remembered like it was yesterday. Of course, it wasn't hard since it was all he ever thought about for the past few years. Even while sleeping, he didn't get a reprieve from the guilt he felt or the pain at the loss of his fellow brothers- and sisters-in-arms.

"James?"

His eyes turned down to the woman in his arms, her hands clung to him like she was the one in need of saving and not the other way around.

"It was me." He licked his lips. His mouth dry as the words fell out of him. "I killed them, seventeen men and eight women, all dead, because of me."

The gasp from her lips and the fear that filled her gaze as she stepped back from him, clenched his heart. Now she would hate him for sure.

"Why?"

The question surprised him. He had expected her to run out screaming, without waiting for an explanation. She should have been turning him in right there but instead, she asked why.

Hands curled into fists, his eyes found her cautious ones. "Why do you think? I'm a monster, a murderer. Why else would I shoot down every single one of them without pause? I should be behind bars or on death row ..."

"Then why aren't you?" she interrupted. "If you are so guilty of these crimes, why are you hiding out here if you know you should be answering for their deaths?" He could see her visibly gulp as she asked her questions, the lawyer in her seeming to overtake any fear she had.

"Because ..." his voice croaked, the emotion billowing up in his chest finally getting to him. "It wasn't me."

"But you just said you killed them." Wendy took a step toward him, and he held his hand up warding her away. She stopped her progression, but didn't stop talking. "You gunned them down one by one, and now you say it wasn't you? Tell me James, how that makes any sense at all."

"Exactly!" He stomped across the room, pausing for a moment before coming back to stand before her. "It doesn't make any sense because when has magic ever made sense to us? I did it, I know I did. I remember the feel of the gun in my hand and the sounds of their cries as I took them out. The ground was littered with bodies and blood. Inside my mind I was trying, I was trying to stop but I couldn't."

James fell to his knees, the stress of retelling his trauma to her too much for him to bear. His shoulders heaved as he tried to hold back the tears threatening to fall. He almost broke when her hands, her tiny hands, touched his shoulders and her voice made shushing sounds in his ear.

"It was Peter, wasn't it? That's why you hate him so much." He felt her kneel beside him, pulling his head into her chest, cradling her to him.

"Yes." Licking his parched lips, he let her hold him.

Normally, in this position he would be trying to get into her pants - she'd left herself open to it - but James felt too raw in that moment to even try. Not since he was a child had anyone held him so tenderly. It was nice to be cared for and not scorned.

"I'm sorry about what I said before, about you not knowing what it was like. I shouldn't have assumed I knew things about you." She lifted his head from her chest, her eyes so warm as she searched his face. "We have more in common than I thought." A slight chuckle left her throat and a sad smile crossed her lips.

"But you see now, don't you?" She held onto his face, her own turning firm. "Why your testimony is even more vital than before? You are proof that it happened to you as well. They can't just believe a soldier randomly turns on his own men the moment they encounter the fae."

"Why not? They already did. Why do you think I'm stuck here?" James scoffed, turning his face from her. "The fae were still new then, there was no precedent for those under magical influence. And I was too ashamed of what I had done to go back."

"But why didn't they come after you? They couldn't forget a whole team of soldiers; they would think something had to have happened?"

Leaning back on his heels, James laughed. "You forget the world we live in, this is the fae world. Anyone who came looking for them was turned around the way they came. They concluded that the team was lost at sea and never made it to the Island."

"Then why are they looking for you? How do they even know you did it?" Wendy's brows furrowed together in that way that made him want to kiss her senseless.

"How do you think? Pan only let me stay on the Island because they needed someone to go between the Island and the mainland. But ever since then, he has been lording it over my head, knowing I can't leave for very long without the chance of someone recognizing me. My last name isn't even Clocker. It's Tinker." James growled his eyes full of vengeful rage.

"Tinker?" The sound of his name on her lips made something in him warm. "If Pan knows you are here and that he could turn you in at any moment, why did he need me to steal something from you?"

"Because he's a right bastard, who just loves to have something over my head. If he had gotten my books he could hand over my schedule to the authorities at any time. It's lucky for me that I take my orders from the council and not that smug prick." James moved to stand, but Wendy grabbed him, pulling him to look at her, a hard determination in her eyes.

"But don't you see? He might have something against you, but you have just as much against him! If you could help me prove that Pan is using magic against humans it would free you from here and you could go anywhere you want."

"Your optimism astounds me." Taking her hands from his face, he pressed his lips to the side of each of them. "But you are right. It's time I stopped hiding and put that little bastard in his place."

"Good. Let's get started." James tightened his hold on her hands as she tried to get up from the floor. "James?"

"Tomorrow." His lips quirked up at her confusion. "We'll work on the case tomorrow. Today," He gave her arms a tug pulling her to him. "Today, you need to be punished for your little stunt earlier."

Bewilderment covered her face, it was so adorable he almost let her get away with it, but he wanted her too badly to let it go. With a wicked smile, he reached into his pocket and presented her with the panties she had dropped not an hour ago.

When she had first dropped them, he had thought it was some kind of accident but when she confirmed it was on purpose, the need that had been building in him had flared to life. He had clutched that thin scrap of fabric she called underwear like it was the last lifeboat on a sinking ship. James would be lying if he said he hadn't thought about jerking off with them, but he decided torturing her would be worth so much more.

The expression on her face, a mixture of horror and embarrassment, proved he was right.

"Punish me?" Her tongue darted out to wet her lips, a hesitant desire and a slight hint of fear in her question. "How?"

"Well, what do you think would be appropriate?" He saw that the request surprised her, her eyes widening a fraction. "Do you always leave your panties where any pervert could take them?"

"No! Of course not." The offended sound of her voice made his lips quirk.

"Then what was the purpose of dropping them where I could get them? Were you trying to play some kind of game? Were you hoping I would come running after inhaling your scent?" He pressed the material to his face, taking in the heady smell of her. If he hadn't already been half way hard, the aroma from the panties was enough to cause him to become painfully so.

"N … no …" she stuttered.

"No? So you weren't trying to tease me? Then what, pray tell, were you trying to do, Wendy?" He turned his head to the side, his voice firm and commanding. When she didn't respond right away, he grabbed her by the back of the thighs, pulling them out from under her, leaving her sprawled out on the floor.

"Nothing, I swear," she cried out as his hands found hers and pinned them above her head. James maneuvered himself between her thighs, and he almost groaned at the heat coming from her. He let his cock rub against the junction of her thin pants, not quite giving either of them enough friction to be satisfied.

Wendy bit her lip as he watched her try not to react to his teasing. That wouldn't do.

He let go of one of her hands to slide it down and cup her breast in his hand, his fingers kneading the mound through her t-shirt.

"Naughty girl, you aren't wearing a bra, are you?" Fingers finding her nipple, he pinched it between them causing her to gasp and moan in response.

"No," her voice rasped and then had the cheek to add, "I'm not wearing panties either."

Surprised by her admission, James glanced down at where their bodies were joined. "Really now?" He rocked his hips slightly, trying to somehow tell if what she was saying was true without removing their clothes.

"Ah." She quivered against him, her hips thrusting up to meet his.

"Now I know you are trying to tease me," James' voice held a dark promise of what would happen if she kept doing what she was doing. He was barely holding on to his control as it was anymore, and he would be fucking her right there on the floor before they even got to the good part.

Ignoring her need, he pressed his hips firmly down onto her keeping her from moving against him. The aggravated roar that ripped through her, made him smile. That was more like it.

His hand went to the hem of her shirt, sliding it up but not touching her skin beneath. Pulling it all the way up until it settled above her breasts, he let his eyes feast on the sight of her pink tipped mounds, each one barely a handful, but plenty enough that he wanted to wrap his lips around them.

Doing just that, James bent his head to take one pert nipple in his mouth. He let his tongue circle around it before pulling it taut with his teeth and then sucked it in deep. Its owner squealed and arched up against him. Satisfied with his work, he switched to the other one, giving it the same treatment. Lick. Pull. Suck.

He kept up that routine while slightly rocking his hips until a strangled word fell from Wendy's mouth.

"What was that? I didn't quite hear you." His mouth hovered over her breasts, his eyes on her thrown back head and the rapid rise and fall of her chest.

"Please," she said again, the word more clear than before, but still strained.

"Please, what?" He pressed his hardened cock against the wetness he could feel pooling through her pants. It was so hot he loved and hated his need to be in control, all he wanted to do was yank her pants down and give them both what they wanted.

"Touch me." Desire and need soaked her words as her back curved into him, trying to get him to move against her.

"You haven't answered my question, why should I give you anything?" When Wendy didn't say anything, James prodded, "Well?" his hips moving so slightly against her the curve of her breast, his hand finding its way to her thigh, using it to lift her higher against him.

"Yes!" she cried out finally. "Yes, I fucking wanted to tease you, you bloody pirate. Now, would you just fuck me?"

Smiling like a lunatic, James released her hands and grasped hold of her hips. "That's a                good                girl."

# CHAPTER 13
## *WENDY*

THE MOMENT HER hands were free she buried them in his hair, pulling his face down to hers. The kiss was the most intense one out of them all. Probably because they were both about to combust with all of his teasing.

Their tongues battled each other, neither wanting to give the other complete control. His mouth pulled at hers, nipping and commanding her to follow his lead, but she was tired of playing by his rules. She wanted him and she wanted him *now*.

The cool floor against her back wasn't enough to deter her from getting him and her both naked. Her hands grabbed at his shirt, tugging and jerking it up and over his head. His eyes laughed at her impatience. She didn't care. Shirt on the ground, her hand found the hard plains of his chest, and she let her hands wander over each muscle, her nails slightly scratching as she went down.

Hands on the waist of his pants, she yanked at them. "Off."

Shaking his head with a smile, he nudged her back down onto the floor. "You first."

Not arguing, she held her breath as his hands found the waistband of her lounge pants. Over and off her, she lay there on the floor completely exposed to his hungry gaze. She tried to sit up to take his pants off next, but he held her down, pushing her thighs even further apart.

When she made a noise of protest, he moved down her body, a smirk on his face until he came face to face with her pussy. Wendy tensed as he just looked at her, not touching her anywhere but where his hand held her legs.

Then a cool breath brushed against her trimmed curls, causing her to bite her lip and groan. Torture. He was bound and determined to torture every inch of pleasure out of her.

"Ever since you dropped your panties, I have been thinking about tasting you." His nose brushed against her, nuzzling her mound.

"James," she gasped, about to tell him to take her already when his tongue lapped up her channel and swirled around her clit. His tongue flattened against her, sliding back and forth over the bundle of nerves that made her toes curl and her hips rise up off the ground.

He circled her once more, building her up to the edge before pulling her tight into his mouth. The sensation caused her to screech and claw at him as she was thrown into the most mind blowing orgasm she had ever experience.

When she could think again, she opened her eyes to find a smug captain staring down at her. Peeved that he could be so unaffected, she sat up from her place on the ground, pushing him backward.

"My turn." Wendy smirked, pulling at his pants until he was the one on the floor with his pants around his ankles.

Stroking up the top of his calves, she took her time feeling the muscles beneath his skin as they flexed against her touch. Her blue eyes peeked up at him from beneath her lashes, watching his face as her fingertips came across his thick thighs and pushed slightly to spread him wide.

Dark hooded eyes looked back at her, watching her every movement. His hands were balled into fists on the ground beside him, as if it was hard to let her be in control. That was good. She liked that she was pushing his limits. Since they'd met, he had always been the one with the leverage. It was nice to finally be the one driving him insane.

Her lips quirked up at that thought, and she deliberately licked her lips. She let herself have a small moment of satisfaction when his eyes locked onto the movement before she dipped her head down to replace her fingertips, trailing her lips along his inner thigh.

A suppressed groan filled her ears as she came just to the edge of his groin before backing off. While her lips pressed open mouth kisses along his skin, her hand reached up and cupped his balls, careful not to touch his engorged cock.

"Wendy." Her name on his lips was a warning that she didn't have much longer of being in charge before he took over.

Not wanting to miss out before she was able to taste him in return, she turned her head, her tongue dipping out to lap up the side of his member. The hardened steel beneath her mouth twitched as she reached the tip, precum glistening on the peak. Wrapping her lips around the top, she savored in the slightly salty taste as she sucked gently on it.

Her other hand gripped the base, moving up and down in time with her sucking. A hand touched the back of her head. She paused, her eyes glancing up to see James' gaze intently on her. His hand loosened the tie in her hair, letting her locks fall around her shoulders. Brushing them to one side of her neck, he held on to it in a firm grip, not pulling, just holding it there. When it seemed like he was ready again, she returned to the task at hand.

Taking more of him into her mouth, she flattened her tongue so that it stroked along the vein at the back of his length. The strangled moan that reverberated out of him told her she was doing something right, so she took him even further into her mouth.

"Fuck." The curse fell from his lips, making her smile around him.

She didn't give head often. Her previous boyfriends had never pressed for it and when she offered they never seemed to complain.

James, on the other hand, didn't have any complaints that he voiced. His hand stayed in her hair, not trying to direct her but more to have something to hold on to besides the floor. When she felt his balls start to tighten, she sped up her movements, licking and swallowing, wanting to push him over that edge like he'd done to her. The hand in her hair stopped her, jerking her off his dick and up to his face where his tongue forced its way into her mouth.

Her breast crushed against the hard plains of his chest, sending shocks of pleasure through her nipples with every movement. Large hands gripped her waist, pulling her into his lap, spreading her legs to either side of him. Instead of sinking her onto his length, he rubbed against the front of her, bringing her to the point of begging.

Digging her hands into his hair, she rocked against him trying to get the friction she needed to reach that peak once more. His hands controlled her movements, speeding up and then slowing right when she was about to be thrown over the edge.

Tired of being denied her release, she nipped at his lips. Her hands clawed at his shoulders, trying to force the captain to give into her demands. But she should have known better than to think he would comply, because as soon as she almost had him inside her, he had them up and off the floor. Then she was being carried across the room.

"What are you doing?" she asked as he dropped her onto the couch, while he walked over to the built in shelving on the wall. Her eyes watched the muscles in his butt flex as he pulled open a drawer and dug around inside.

"Do you trust me?" He looked over his shoulder at her, eyes glinting with promise as his hand touched something in the drawer.

Fingers gripping the side of the couch, her body thrummed from the lack of release. His eyes on her made her squirm, and before she could think too much about it, she found herself saying, "Yes."

Her eyes zeroed in on his hand as it lifted something up and out of the drawer. When she realized what was in his hands, her heart beat sped up and her thighs pressed together in anticipation.

It was a red nylon rope, the nice quality kind. Not the kind of rope she would expect on a cargo ship. The sight of it scared and exhilarated her.

"Have you been tied up before?" He sauntered toward her, unwinding the cord from around itself.

Gulping at the sight of his hands going to work. So practiced. So deliberate. He'd done this before.

"No." Her voice shook and she cleared her throat, forcing herself to look him in the eye. "I mean, not really. I've used those fuzzy handcuffs people get you as gag gifts, but well, those never really work right." She gave a nervous chuckle but it caught in her throat at the intensity of his gaze.

"This is different," he explained. James paused before her so the rope was at the level of her gaze, only slightly overshadowed by his still-erect cock pressing against his stomach.

"Yeah," she muttered, and then glanced up at him. "Will you spank me?"

"I hadn't planned on it, but I could." He chuckled and a dangerous smile tipped his lips. "Would you like me to?"

"No," she said quickly with a shake of her head and then added when he frowned. "I mean, yes, I would, but not now."

The thought of having his hand against her backside made her cheeks tingle in remembrance. She had enjoyed it, yes, and she would like to have it happen again. Preferably with an orgasm at the end, but right now she wanted nothing more than to have him inside her, and spanking would just make it a longer more torturous wait.

"All right." He simply nodded and then turned, gesturing to the center of the office, where a rug lay. "Kneel over there."

Standing on shaky legs, she stalked across the floor making sure to add an extra swing to her hips. Wendy could feel his eyes burning into her skin as she kneeled on the rug. She had been worried the rug would be rough against her knees. It was softer than it looked, and made part of her want to roll around on it.

"Put your hands behind your back." His voice commanded just inches from behind her.

Placing one arm and then the other behind her back, she jumped a little when his warm hand wrapped around her bicep. He wrapped the rope around both of her arms and went to work on trussing her up. She couldn't stand the silence and asked the question that had been plaguing her since he pulled the rope out of his drawer.

"So, do you do this often?" She winced as the question sounded bitter and not curious like she had hoped.

"No, not really." His hands kept moving while he talked, her biceps being bound together but not pinching or hurting.

"I thought maybe you had, why else would you keep things like this in your office." She gave a little chuckle and rolled her eyes at her own words. She sounded like a jealous girlfriend.

He didn't seem to notice and kept working on her arms. "Most people come to the island to be with the fae, not a cargo ship captain." He tugged on the rope, causing her to jerk a tiny bit. "Though, every once in a while a straggler finds their way into my ship. Though, none of them have tried to steal from me before." The laughter in his voice made her turn to look over her shoulder, to find him staring at her intently. "Comfortable?"

Thinking about it, she tried to move her arms. The ropes were tight but not so tight it bit into her skin, just enough that she couldn't move them but she wouldn't have to worry about losing the circulation in her arms. The more she moved though, the less balance she seemed to have and she would've face planted into the floor had James' hand not come up to steady her.

"Alright?" he asked, his hands caressing her shoulders and down to her arms, a shiver ran along her skin where he touched her and she nodded. "If you want to stop we can, just say the word."

"What word?" she cocked her head back to see him, though it was difficult at that position. "Isn't there usually a safe word in these kinds of situations?"

She definitely needed a safe word. Being restrained with some flimsy plastic handcuffs was one thing, but this was no passing fancy. This was big league bondage, the kind that required a certain amount of trust between partners. Something she wasn't sure had enough of to not have a way out.

There was no need to worry though, because James gave her a proud and reassuring smile. "So you do know a little bit." He placed a hand on the back of her head leaning it back so his lips could ghost over hers. "The word is Tinker."

"Tinker?" she pulled back from his lips. "But won't that be weird having the safe word be your last name?"

Having a safe word made her feel better, but only slightly. Her heart still hammered in her chest at the thought of being at his mercy, even as her inner walls screamed for him to take her already.

"No." He shook his head. "No one else knows that name but you, so no matter how out of my mind I am, and I have no doubt you will drive me there," He nipped at her shoulder with his teeth, leaving a sharp tingle in its wake. "I am always on the alert for anyone saying that name."

"All right, Tinker it is." She nodded. Facing the desk a few feet away from them, she waited for him to tell her what to do next. The quiet in the room was deafening and made her anxiety skyrocket. Not liking his silence, she glanced back at him again. "Now what?"

"Now." His hands grabbed a hold of her rope covered arms, slowly pressing her down until her face touched the floor. "I'm going to fuck you."

Cheek against the rug and her ass in the air, she never felt so exposed. Or excited. Not being able to move or get away frightened her. She was a control freak at heart and letting anyone have this much control of her body was not something she could easily give up. James was different, though.

They hadn't known each other long but she felt like she could trust him, to an extent. Especially after he opened up about what had happened to him and why he was there. So having herself in such a vulnerable position made her quake with excitement, with just a hint of fear making it that much better.

"You have such a lovely ass, you know that?" His hand slid along her cheek before smacking it once, sending a ring of pain through her. "I know you said no spanking, but that will be the only one, I promise." His voice was deep and concentrated as his hands swept over her backside and down her spine, his erection pressing against her folds.

"Do you have any idea how many times I've imagined you like this?" He rocked his hips against her so his cock became slick from her wetness. "That first time I had my hands on you," he groaned, "it took everything I had not to fuck you right then and there."

Small sounds came out of her with every movement of his hips. The ridges of his cock slid across her clit, building up the pressure that had subsided while they talked. Now she was soaking, and more than ready for him to be inside of her.

"Please," she whined, pressing her butt back against him.

"You're ready for me aren't you, sweetheart?" He reached a hand down and flicked her bundle of nerves before sliding a finger inside her.

She clenched around the intrusion, rocking her hips so she moved on his finger. He let her ride his finger for a moment before pressing another one inside and she gave a deep moan at the full feeling.

"You're so fucking perfect, Wendy." His fingers fucked her, forcing tiny cries from her lips. It felt so good but she wanted more. She wanted him.

"James!" She buried her face in the rug. "Please."

Removing his fingers, she felt hollow and empty inside but screamed when his cock took their place. His hips pressed against hers while he fully sheathed himself in her. He didn't move at first, letting her adjust to his size. He was bigger than she imagined, and the angle she was at made it so much deeper than she had ever had before. It was almost on the side of painful.

"How are you doing?" he asked, his breathing labored and strained.

She nodded, but then spoke up when she realized he probably couldn't see the small movement. "I'm fine. Please keep going."

"Okay, hold on." The humor in his words was not lost on her, but she couldn't get a giggle out before he was pulling back and then sliding back into her.

Each slap of his hips against her sent rivets of pleasure throughout her body. At first she tried to push back, not wanting him to do all the work, but eventually, it was easier just to let him be in control and drive them both into oblivion.

Every stroke brought her that much closer to the edge, and he was so deep she wasn't sure she would be able to take it much longer. The safe word was on her lips when his hand slipped between her thigh, rubbing over her clit and tossing her into an orgasm that had her seeing spots. He wasn't far behind, because he grabbed the ropes holding her arms and pulled her up against him as he roared out his release.

When they finished, James untied her arms so quick she collapsed. His arm caught her, and he eased them both to the ground. Their breathing was labored as they lay in the afterglow of their lovemaking.

Love making? Her eyes opened at the thought. Since when had it become that? She admitted she was growing quite attached to the captain, but she wouldn't call it love. Not yet at least. Besides, she didn't even know how he felt about her. It had been barely more than a day since they'd met and while a lot had happened in that time, it would be crazy to call that love.

James must have felt her stiffen. His hands stroked her back in a soothing manner. "What's wrong?"

Turning on her side, she faced him with a smile. "Nothing. Just thinking about when we could do that again."

"Again?" he laughed. "Let me catch my breath first woman, and then I'll see what I can do."

"Out of shape, old man?" She poked at him, smirking at his widened eyes.

"Old man?" he mocked. "I'll show you old man."

Wrapping his arms around her waist, she giggled as she let him draw her into a kiss she was sure would end with her liquefied corpse on the floor.

# Chapter 14
## *James*

WHEN HE WOKE the next morning, it was a struggle to get out of bed. His body seemed a hundred times its weight and more than a little reluctant to leave the warmth of the delicious creature next to him. Thinking of Wendy, James thought back to the night before.

The attraction between them was out of this world. He swore he had shot through the roof and into the sky with how hard he had come. The second time he took her on the rug was just as good. The memory of her breasts bouncing as she moved above him made him harden.

After another explosion that made both their eyes roll into their heads, they had snuck back to his room. They laughed and whispered so the crew didn't catch them as they ran down the hall buck-ass naked.

When they arrived at his bedroom, and behind closed doors, they were all over each other again. Hands stroking skin, lips and tongues finding any piece of flesh they could get a hold of. Then they had collapsed on the bed, where he slowly entered her. This time was different. They took their time as they achingly progressed to their final orgasm of the night, both passing out soon afterward.

A small smile crept up his face. It had been one of the best nights of his life. He wasn't sure he would ever be able to let it go.

James slid an arm around Wendy's waist, pressing his length against the swell of her butt. His fingers reached up to cup her breast. Still asleep, she let out a sigh and pressed her bottom against him, not seeming to know her grinding was driving him wild.

His hand traveled down from her breast, along her stomach, to dip in between her thighs where she was hot and ready for him. Pressing down on her clit, he thrust his hips against her while she moaned underneath his ministration.

"Again?" her sleep voice croaked at him as she opened her legs wider for him to slip his fingers into her.

"Always." He sped up his hand until she was writhing against him. She was always so wet for him. He couldn't imagine a more perfect woman for him. When she was just on the edge, he removed his fingers to pick her legs up and eased himself into her gripping embrace.

It didn't take long for James to find his release, and he let out a low groan as Wendy clamped down on him, riding out her own.

"Wow." Wendy sighed, her head thrown back onto the pillow. "I don't think I will ever get tired of that."

"I would hope not." His lips curled up as he looked down at her. Hair splayed across his pillow, her brown eyes still not quite awake, she was the most beautiful thing he had ever seen.

Pink lips returned his smile and a giggle sounded from her before she shifted as if to get out of bed. Not having any of it, James grabbed her retreating form and pressed her back into the mattress. He maneuvered between her thighs, holding her there.

"You can't be ready again. I'm starting to think you aren't quite human?" Wendy's words would have upset him had it not been for the twinkle in her eyes.

"I'm as human as they come, you on the other hand..." He let his finger trail down her breast, holding the weight in his hand. "... could very well be a witch, because you have more than bespelled me." James leaned down to capture her mouth in his, his cock waking up once more.

"You're insatiable." She laughed, pushing him off of her.

He moved away letting her get up from the bed, not hating the view of her naked body standing in his bedroom. Hips that had just the right amount of curve, and a waist that was tiny, but still held a womanly figure. James couldn't get enough of her.

"Come on." She tossed a discarded pillow at him. "Get up. We have work to do you horny pirate."

"Work?" he groaned. "Who can think about work when the sea goddess herself prances around my room looking so tempting?"

"Flattery will get you nowhere with me, good sir." Wendy's face was serious, though, he could see her fighting a smile.

He leaned on his elbow as he watched her move about the room, picking up things here and there. It was strange to have a woman in his room, even more so one that he hadn't kicked out already. James hadn't been lying when he said he rarely did these kinds of things. It was even rarer for him to find someone who was even into a bit of bondage. Most women were so wary of just getting a spanking, they didn't know that with every pain comes even more pleasure, and James didn't have the patience to teach them.

Wendy, though, she was someone he wanted around long enough to show all the delights his tastes had in store. He already knew she enjoyed some of it, and the delightful red color that stained her skin when it was pressed to its limit was something he would never get tired of seeing.

"Are you going to stay in bed all day?" Her voice pulled him out of his thoughts. He eyed her standing by the bathroom door.

"It depends. Is there anything worth doing outside of this big warm bed that smells so much like you?" he smirked at the pink that crept up her face. He loved that he could embarrass her so easily. It made him think of all the different ways he could get her to blush.

"Well, if you are a good little sailor, I may let you wash my back." She returned his smirk with a teasing grin and a sashay of her hips that had him up and out of bed in no time.

"I'm up," he said, darting after her and into the bathroom. He could definitely get used to this.

"SO, I WAS thinking about what we really need for this to work," Wendy stated later while looking over the files she had told him her friend had sent her.

"What's that?" He stopped tapping his pen on his desk and glanced to where she sat next to him, her computer set up next to his own.

Pulling away from her laptop, she turned to James. "While both of us have been under Peter's magic, our stories would be more believable if we had anyone there to prove that was what was happening. But it isn't likely that any of the other fae or tourists, for that matter, will be stepping up anytime soon to help us out. So, what we really need is someone still in Peter's control."

"And where are we going to find one of those? It's not like they are waltzing around Never Isles just waiting for us to pick them up." He gestured out the office porthole.

"No, but I do know where one is." James frowned at the mischievous look in her eye, not at all liking where her mind was going. It spelled trouble and not the kind he liked out of the bedroom.

THE BAR WENDY took him to was the Hideaway Bar. James knew very well this was the hangout place for Pan and his miscreants. He made a point to stay away from it, same as the rest of the locals.

"What are we doing here?" He grabbed her elbow, stopping her from going into the bar. "This isn't exactly keeping a low profile."

Hands on her hips, Wendy scowled. "We don't really have much of a choice now do we? Lily is in there. I'm sure of it, and if she is as far gone as I think, she will be perfect for our case."

"That's if we can get her to come with us," he pointed out, putting his hands in his pocket. "How do you know she won't call Pan and all his idiot friends down on us while we are in the bowels of their operation? I know I won't be bespelled by Pan, but I'm worried he might get to you again or one of the others." Placing his hands on her shoulders, he drew her to him.

She had just come into his life and already he was attached. He knew what his life was like before the smart-mouthed lawyer snuck into his ship, and he didn't want to go back to that lonely existence.

Her hands gripped his back holding on to him just as tightly. "Don't worry, it will be fine. Besides ..." She pulled back with a cheeky grin. "... if I get bespelled, you will just have to make sure to spank it out of me again."

"Oh, I will be spanking something, though, it may not be your delectable ass," he growled, capturing her lips with his for a quick kiss before ushering them into the dimly lit bar.

The place was abandoned, which wasn't a surprise since it was barely eight o'clock in the morning, and anyone in a bar that early usually hadn't been to bed yet, or was an alcoholic. Pan and his gang weren't either of those.

"It's quiet," Wendy murmured, her eyes searching the bar. While it had been her idea, he could see how tense she was about being there, her hands were balled into fists and her shoulders bunched up around her neck. It was like she was waiting for them to jump out at any moment, shouting, "Boo!"

"That's a good thing." James took her hand in his, leading her toward the back door. "We don't want them to be here, remember?"

Through the doorway, he led them down a dark hallway, Wendy's hand clutched his own. His heart swelled with emotion at the way she depended on him to keep her safe. He tightened his grip on hers, his eyes narrowing as they came into a red lit room. He wouldn't let anyone hurt her, she wouldn't turn out like his comrades, or he would do more than take Pan to court.

"Hello?" a small voice called from the other side of the room, on a thin dingy mattress. "Peter?"

Before James could respond, Wendy let go of his hand and jogged over to where the voice had come from. As he approached the bed after her, he noticed a dark haired girl. She had to be barely over twenty-one and scantily dressed in a tiny sheer dress. Even in the dim lighting, he could see the dark circles under her eyes and the strain on her face. There was desperation in her eyes that he knew were signs of Pan's spell.

"Lily?" Wendy kept a low soothing voice as she knelt next to the mattress. "We are here to help you. Why don't you come with us, and we can get you something to eat and maybe some new clothes to wear? Peter would like that, don't you think? You could look pretty for him."

The girl glanced at him and Wendy as if trying to decide if they were really there on Pan's behalf. He almost thought they had her when she stood up from the mattress but jumped forward when she reached out to hit Wendy.

"Bitch!" the girl snarled. "I remember you from last time. You tried to hurt my Peter."

James held onto the girl as she tried to get around him to attack Wendy. She bit and clawed at anything she could get a hold of, shouting curses and calling them names.

"We're trying to help you! You don't know what he has done to you. He's not a good man." Wendy tried to reason with her, but it only made Lily more furious.

"You don't know what you are talking about, he's great! He's wonderful. Peter takes care of me. I love him, and he would never leave me. Not even for a snotty bitch like you." She faked going left and tried to get around James. He grabbed her around the waist and hauled her over his shoulder.

Turning to Wendy, he frowned. "How are we going to get her out of her without drawing attention to ourselves?"

"Here." Wendy grabbed a piece of the sheet from the bed and ripped it. Tying the girl's hands, she went for another piece, which she balled up and shoved in the screeching girl's mouth. "It's not perfect, but it will at least eliminate some of the hassle. We better get moving before her yelling brings in curious early birds."

James followed Wendy as she led them out of the room and into the bar. Still deserted, they booked it for the door. Sticking her head out of the bar door, she popped back in, motioning him the coast was clear.

They made their way out of the bar and across the beach where a few early risers gave them curious looks, but didn't do anything to help the tied up girl. It would have been disheartening had James not been the one kidnapping her in the first place.

When they were safely behind his office doors, James plopped their prisoner into a chair and grabbed the rope from last night's play. He quickly tied her to the chair around the middle, while Wendy held her down with her hands on her shoulders.

"Didn't think you'd be committing a crime when you came to the island, did you?" James smiled at her over the squirming girl.

"It's not a crime," she protested. "We're helping her, even if she doesn't know it yet." When James finished tying the knots, Wendy let go of Lily's shoulders and came around to the front of her. "Besides, we need her, and there wasn't any other way to get proof."

Crossing his arms over his chest, he looked down at the girl. Pathetically covered in a slip of a dress, she glared up at them as if they were scum beneath her feet. Wendy was right, they really didn't have a choice. He had done the exact same thing to her not forty-eight hours ago, and he'd do it again to save anyone stuck under that vile creatures spell.

The only question was. "What do we do with her now?"

# CHAPTER 15
## *WENDY*

PACING BACK AND forth over the hard floors of James' office, a mild panic attack was making its way through Wendy's body. Her feet made a thud-thud that went along to the rising beat of her heart.

They'd kidnapped a person. A person! She was a lawyer for fuck's sake. She was supposed to be preventing crimes, not committing them. Her hands dug into her hair as she twisted it tight in her grip, trying to figure out how she had gotten so far.

Head down, she ignored the daggers directed toward her from their captive and James who was watching her from his desk.

Usually, his eyes on her made her skin tingle and body ache, but right now it only made her anxiety shoot through the roof.

"Wendy," his voice, a soothing timber, made her pause in mid-stride.

"What?" she snapped, before resuming her trek across the floor.

"As much as I love to watch your tight ass in those jeans, you need to calm down." He stood and rounded his desk, stopping in front of her to place his hands on her shoulders. "What's done is done, and we aren't doing anything wrong."

"But we kidnapped someone! How is that not wrong?" Wendy's voice broke off in a panicked screech.

A muffled voice reminded her they weren't exactly alone. Turning to their prisoner, Wendy reached out and pulled the strip of torn up sheet out of Lily's mouth.

"Bitch! Let me go or Peter is going to make you pay when he finds out I'm gone." Her dark hair whipped around her as she snarled and yelled at them before Wendy shoved the material back into her mouth. What had she gotten herself into?

"See!" James pointed at her. "She's clearly under Pan's power. Would you really want to leave her with him? And what about the case? Like you said, we won't have a chance in hell if we don't have proof and here we have it, proof."

Wendy chewed on her lips, looking between Lily and James. He was right, they did need her, and it had been her idea. But how were they going to get her to the courtroom without calling attention to themselves? Even if they got back to the mainland, they couldn't very well take her through town, and it would take a while to get a court hearing, even one for such a severe case such as Lily's.

"Fine, but we need to get back to Florida as soon as possible." Wendy crossed her arms over her chest, thinking of all the things she needed to do to get their case filed and expedited as fast as possible. "I'll have to find somewhere to get the paperwork set up and a judge that would even see our case. Problem is, what do we do with her until then? If we untie her she'll just try to escape."

"Let's worry about one thing at a time." James drew her to him, wrapping his arms around her waist. "Now getting to Florida? Not a problem. We have a shipment that is due in Miami today, so we could be underway in the next hour."

"Miami?" Her eyes widened. "That would be perfect! My old job has an office there that handles cases like this specifically." Wendy couldn't contain the excitement in her voice as she realized she might not have to go at it alone. Surely there was someone there that she could utilize to help get their case through.

"All right then, let's get moving. I'll get Smith to make sure we are ready to lift anchor and the men are all back. You can ..." he trailed off, looking toward Lily. Her deep, black eyes held so much hate that it caused Wendy to be sick to her stomach.

What kind of person was she before Peter had gotten a hold of her? What would happen to her when they finally got the spell off her? And would she ever be the same girl she was before she came to the Island?

All these questioned piled up in her, and she ached for the girl. No matter what she would do whatever it took to get Lily out of Peter's spell and back to any semblance of normal she could.

The question was — would she thank her for it?


JAMES HAD HELPED Wendy move Lily into his bathroom, where she had set up a bath. While she was sure that Peter probably kept her fed well enough, he didn't really seem to care much about her hygiene. Or maybe Lily was just too far gone to bother being away from Peter for very long?

Either way, her hair was greasy and she had dirt under her nails. The clothing she wore, a tiny dress that barely covered her butt, was stained and in dire need of a wash —or a blow torch.

They'd untied her once they got her into the tub. James brought out the handcuffs he'd used on her before and latched her to the railing next to the tub. It probably wasn't the most comfortable position but at least she couldn't run away.

The gag, Wendy had contemplated leaving in because she really didn't want to listen to her curse and yell at her while she tried to help her clean up. But the girl's mouth was probably getting tired and dry from the cloth gag, and if her clothing had been disgusting the sheet from the mattress probably wasn't any better.

"Here." Turning toward the sound of James' voice, Wendy's eyebrows shot up. In his hand was a leather gag that wrapped around the wearer's head and had a plastic black bar across one side like a horses bit. "In case she becomes too hard to handle."

"And you just had this laying around, did you?" She tentatively took the gag from his hand, sitting it on the counter next to her. Just looking at it made her feel funny, the thought of actually using it was unthinkable.

James shrugged his shoulders, not at all embarrassed by her question. "Among other things."

"And these other things, are they like this?" her eyes snapped to Lily who made a rude noise in her throat, but thankfully didn't comment.

"Would you like to find out?" There was a glint in James' eyes when he smiled at her, one that made her panties wet and her nipples tighten.

Mouth dry, Wendy coughed, clearing her throat. "Um, maybe later." She glanced over at Lily, who watched them delightfully amused as embarrassment covered Wendy's face. It would have been annoying had it not been the first time the girl hadn't been glaring at them.

"I'll hold you to it." Grinning, he kissed the top of her head and then headed out of the bathroom.

A silly smile on her lips, she turned back to Lily, whose amusement had fallen and was back to shooting daggers at her. Frowning, she picked up the scissors and eyed Lily who gave her an evil smirk as if she was just daring Wendy to get those near her.

Jesus Christ, what was she thinking?

AN HOUR AND one drenched lawyer later, Wendy got Lily as clean as she could with the handcuffs making Lily's dress hang off one arm and her attacking her at every opportunity. Not even five minutes into it, and she had been wishing she'd asked James to stay. Currently, she was trying to get the stubborn girl to get out of the bathtub on her own, but she refused to do anything she said.

"When Peter gets here, just you wait. He will destroy you for being mean to his lily pad." She stuck her lip out in a pout.

Lily pad? Wendy shook her head in disgust and to think this could be her.

Throwing the towel over the girl's nude form, she grabbed another one as she leaned against the sink to dry off her clothes. She needed to get information from the little hellion, but if all she did was fight and cry, Wendy didn't think she was going to be able to get anything out of her. Not unless she suddenly had red hair and a penis.

"Why did you take me anyways?"

Wendy stopped drying her hair at the unexpected question. "Why?"

"Yes." Lily sat up in the tub, using the towel to dry off what she could with one hand. "I don't know you, except what I've discerned in the last few hours and the one other time you came to the bar. So, why would you even care about me? I'm nobody."

"But you were somebody at one time before you came to the Never Isles?" Now that she got her talking, she wasn't about to let a good opportunity go to waste. "Is your name really Lily?"

"Why wouldn't it be?" she rolled her dark eyes and stepped out of the tub.

Shrugging, she went on to another question. "So, where did you live before?"

"Before?" Lily dropped the towel, not caring that she was completely nude in front of a stranger. "You mean before Peter saved me?"

"Saved you? Is that what he did?" Wendy tried hard not to scoff in disbelief. The thought of Peter saving anyone was so out there that she expected her to claim the fae could also fly.

"Of course!" Lily's eyes lit up. "I came here to run away, like all of us do." She eyed Wendy knowingly. "And that's when Peter found me. He said I was the most beautiful thing he had ever seen and someone so gorgeous shouldn't be crying over ... well, what I had been crying over. I don't really remember what it was now. It seems so long ago now."

"Do you remember how long it was?" she held her breath as she waited to hear what Lily would say.

"Uh ..." She bent over drying her hair, her eyes kind of glazed over as she thought about it. "I'm not really sure, time doesn't work the same here and with Peter, well — time doesn't really matter when he's around."

"So, you don't know how old you are?" Wendy's eyes widened.

"I guess I don't, but who really cares about stuff like that?" Lily shrugged, her wet hair plastered to the back of her shoulders.

Nodding, Wendy chewed her lip as she thought. How could someone not know how old they were? From where Wendy sat, the girl could barely be more than twenty-one. With no idea how long she'd been there it would make it hard to present the severity of their case to the courts. There had to be some way to figure it out.

"What about your family? Friends? Didn't anyone come looking for you?"

Lily gave her a disgusted look. "What family? I was a foster kid until I was sixteen. That's when I made my way here to the Never Isles. Where nothing bad could ever happen, and look?" She held her hands out around her. "Here I am happy and in love with the leader of the whole Island. Tell me how could that be wrong?"

# CHAPTER 16
## *JAMES*

SMITH WAS HANDING him the last of the paperwork that needed to be signed before they shipped off when Peter Pan came stomping up his ramp. Gone was the usual smug grin and in its place was a nasty snarl, contorting his boyish features into the monster he was.

"Where is she?" He stopped in front of James, his nose inches away from his face.

"You have so many women I couldn't possibly know who you are talking about." James turned from him to sign the form, so Smith could scamper off.

"Don't fuck with me, Clocker." Pan shoved a finger into his chest, James tried not to smile when his finger hit pure muscle and a slight wince crinkled the side of his eye. "I know you have her. One of the shopkeepers saw you and that British bitch go into the bar this morning. And now I can't find Lily anywhere."

"You actually know her name?" James smirked. "I thought you just named them by the day of the week you were fucking them on."

He felt it the moment Pan's rage skyrocketed. The air became heavy and electric. An incessant urge to bow down to the fae pressed down on him, making it feel like gravity had quadrupled in size. But James knew it wasn't real, it was an illusion meant to make him bend to the redhead's will and he wasn't having it.

His fist tightened around the pen in his hand until the metal clip bit into his skin. As his mind registered the pain, the air became lighter and the need to serve disappeared. The shock, and then anger, on Pan's face were priceless.

Grinning like a maniac, James stepped toward him and his smile grew even bigger when the fae backed up. "As you can see, your magic doesn't work on me anymore. So, why don't you save yourself an ass whipping —God knows I don't need a reason - and get the hell off my ship."

Pan stumbled back, something like fear on his face. It took everything in James not to bait him more, but at that moment, Wendy came rushing out onto the deck, her face flushed and full of excitement.

"You'll never believe what I found out!" she cried out, not seeming to have noticed their guest. "I couldn't get much and don't even ask how the bath went but —"

"Sweetheart, now is not a good time," he interrupted her, his eyes darting from her to Pan, who was still standing on the edge of the ship, his fear transformed into to a cocky grin.

Wendy's eyes went from James to Pan, and her mouth snapped shut.

"No, please, Wendy. Do tell us what you found out?" Pan's voice held a different kind of magic that James had luckily never had directed toward him but he could tell by Wendy's face that it was having the desired effect.

James took the few steps it took to get to her side, pulled his hand back and swung it down with a hard whack. Wendy jumped in place. The glaze in her eyes cleared and she grabbed a hold of James' arm, glaring at the smug fae.

"I knew I should have fucked you the moment I saw you. Tell me is she as good a lay as she looks? They always say the tighter wound they are, the wilder they are in the sack."

James snarled taking a step toward him, but Wendy held him back as Pan laughed.

"That's right, honey, keep him in check. But he can't protect you from me forever. Eventually, I will get to her, and then I will take you and the little bitch down." With an evil laugh, Pan turned his back on them, then made his way down and off the ship's ramp.

The moment he was out of sight, James hollered for Smith.

"Yes, Capt'n?" he stuttered.

"Is the crew ready?" James asked, clutching Wendy closer to his side.

"Just about, we are still waiting on a few stragglers." Smith looked down at the clipboard in his hands.

"Well, get your butt on the phone and tell them they have ten minutes to get here or we leave without them," James demanded, his eyes trained on where Pan had been not a few seconds ago.

"Bu ... but, Capt'n, there's no way they'll be able to get here that fast. Some live on the other side of the island," his first mate sputtered over himself as he tried to explain.

"I don't care, make it happen. We need to leave now." James turned his back on the man, directing Wendy back below deck.

He brought them into his office and didn't stop until the door was firmly closed behind him. Taking Wendy into his arms, he pressed his mouth to hers, needing to taste her to calm his raging heart.

Her mouth opened to him. Her hands grasped his shirt, pulling him closer to her. Groaning at her response, one hand came up to cup the back of her neck while the other one got a handful of her delectable backside. The anger he had felt for Pan morphed into another emotion that caused his cock to stiffen against her stomach.

Lifting her up by the back of her thighs until her legs were wrapped around his waist, he moved them across the room until he had her sitting on the top of his desk. Wendy pulled back, taking a deep labored breath, her chest rising and falling so that his eyes drew down to her breasts.

"Hold on we need to talk about what I found out." Her hands went to his shoulders, giving him a little push.

"You talk." His fingers worked open her jeans, sliding them down her legs. "I play."

"That's not very product—" James' hand slid inside of her panties cutting her words off. His fingers trailed up and down her slit, spreading her wetness around before pressing down on her clit.

"What were you saying?" James asked, his lips finding the side of her neck.

A moan was his only response as his fingers worked her body. Wendy ground against his hand as he left her bundle of nerves to slip his fingers inside her, inwardly groaning at the clench of her walls.

"When you came out on the deck talking, I thought we were done for," he continued, his mouth still against the side of her neck, gliding his lips up and down the column. "Unfortunately, Pan was right. I won't always be there to smack you out of it." He popped her on the backside causing her hips to move even faster again him.

"How can I do that?" Her words were needy, but inquisitive.

"Pain," Removing his hand from her, he pulled her panties down her thighs until they fell to the floor. He lifted her legs over his shoulders as he released himself from the confines of his pants, "is, as you remember, an easy way to snap out of a spell." He eased inside of her, both of them moaning in unison.

"How did you do it?" Hands gripping the edge of the desk as he pounded into her, her words came out in short spurts. "Who smacks your ass?"

Grinning down at the slight smile on her face as she asked her question, James picked up his speed almost punishing her for her words. Loving the sound of her cries of pleasure, James leaned down until his lips brushed her ear. "Nobody spanks this captain."

WHEN THEY'D BOTH reached their completion, James sat in his desk chair with Wendy nestled on top of his lap. The more he was around her, the more he couldn't get enough of her. She never backed down when he challenged her. She was smart, kind-hearted — she had proved as much with how she'd reacted to his story — and she was so gorgeous that he hardly believed she was real.

"So, what were you coming to tell me before?" James lifted his head from on top of hers.

"Oh." Her head rose from his chest, her eyes meeting his. "I got Lily to open up a bit while giving her a bath. Which by the way was not fun at all. That girl bites." She grimaced at the memory.

Chuckling, James smiled. "I'd imagine not."

"Anyways." She rolled her eyes at him. "She wouldn't tell me because she doesn't seem to remember much between now and when Peter first bespelled her."

"That's normal. Usually, those ensnared by the fae are in a trance-like state the majority of the time and barely remember one hour to the next, let alone long spans of time. It's only when they finally come to their senses that they start to fill in the blanks." At the shocked expression on her face, James added, "It's the mind's way of coping with whatever atrocities that are being forced on them. Though, having it come back all at once at the end probably isn't doing them any favors."

"No, I wouldn't think so." She spoke quietly, as if in thought. "You know, it's no wonder that most of the cases I read said that most of the people taken by the fae ended up in a psychiatric hospital, or end up with severe PTSD."

The shiver that went through her had James pulling her close to him, his lips touching her forehead. "That won't ever happen to you. I've got you, sweetheart, and I won't let that bastard touch you."

"I know, but I was thinking about Lily." She gave a disheartened sigh. "I'm afraid it might be too late for her. She doesn't remember how long she's been here, but she remembered how old she was when she arrived."

She was quiet for a second and James had to look down at her to see that her eyes were still open.

"She was sixteen, James. Sixteen."

Her words made James' blood boil. The fact that Pan was taking women as sex slaves was bad enough but taking a minor? Unforgivable.

"He'll pay, Wendy. We will make him pay. In court, or out of court. He won't be able to take another man, woman, or child against their will ever again." The murderous tone of his voice should have warned him he was on a dangerous path, but it only solidified the need to have the bastard behind bars, or in the ground.

Before Wendy could respond, a knock came at the office door.

"Capt'n." Smith's voice came from the other side. "We're ready to cast off."

“Good.” James lifted Wendy off his lap. “It’s time to get this plan in motion.”

194

# CHAPTER 17
## *WENDY*

A TWINGE OF jealousy ran through Wendy as she watched James tie up their prisoner in his office chair. It wasn't Lily's fault really. She couldn't help that she was taller and had more curves than Wendy. When they found she was too big to fit into any of her clothes it was only probable that she would have to borrow some of James. But sitting there watching her in one of his t-shirts as it stretched against her generous bust, Wendy couldn't keep back the resentful need to claw the girl's eyes out.

"There, that should hold her." He tugged on the rope showing Wendy the girl was good and restrained. The same rope he had used on *her* the other night.

Growling at her own silliness, Wendy stood from the couch. "As soon as we dock, I need to go to shore. There's a branch of my old firm there that I'm going to utilize. Hopefully, it will get our case before a judge faster."

She didn't look at James as she gathered her things and made for the door. Before she got more than two steps into the hallway, though, his hands clamped down on her arm, pulling her back.

"Hey," he said, his voice low and soothing. "What's wrong?"

"Nothing." She sighed. "I'm just tired is all. I just wanted it to be over, you know? Get Peter behind bars — or whatever they do with fae, and Lily to where she can get some help."

James glanced down at her, a knowing look on his face. "I feel like there is more to it than that."

"No, there's not." Her lip stuck out in a pout.

"It bothered you, didn't it?" He wrapped his arms around her waist, drawing her to him.

"What did?" Wendy sunk into his embrace, breathing him in. He always smelled of the sea and his own flavor of man. She could bottle it and sell it for a fortune if she could bear the thought of another woman having his scent.

"Seeing me tie Lily up with our rope." His hand stroked the line of her back, causing the muscles in her shoulders to sag. "I have others you know. Ones you haven't seen yet."

"But that's *our* rope." She winced at the whine in her voice.

James chuckled, the feel of it reverberating through her, making her toes curl. "Would you like me to go use something else? I can, it wouldn't take long."

"Could you?" Wendy asked, but quickly shook her head. "No, never mind. It's silly to go to all the trouble when you've already finished."

"Are you sure?"

"Yes, it's fine, really." Her eyes met his with a smile. "Besides, I have to get going."

"All right, if you say so." His lips quirked up in that half-smile that made her insides liquefy.

Pushing up on her tiptoes, she eased her arms around his neck, pressing her lips to his. Instead of letting him direct their kiss, she pushed all of herself into it. Nipping and licking at his mouth until they were both breathless and aching for more, Wendy swelled with pride at his hooded gaze staring back at her.

"What was that for?" His voice was scratchy, and he cleared his throat, asking his question again.

"Nothing." It was her turn to smirk. "Just something to think about while I'm gone."

"Oh, I'll be thinking about it all right." Wendy yelped when he swatted her on the rump. "And how pretty and pink your ass will look bent over my desk."

Excitement filled her at the prospect of him spanking her again. It was still new to her to mix pleasure with pain, but the more they did it, the more she craved it. If someone had asked her a month ago if she was into BDSM she would have laughed in their faces, but now because of this delicious man, she couldn't imagine going back to plain old vanilla.

"Then we both have something to think about." Her voice was breathy as she clutched her paperwork to her chest, taking a step back. She couldn't trust herself to keep her hands to herself and not continue what *she* had started. Going to the mainland seemed less important now.

THE BELL ABOVE the door chimed as she stepped out of the humid Miami air, and into the tiny, but thankfully air-conditioned office. Darlings and Darlings, L.L.P. had five firms. One in New York where the brothers primarily worked. Then there was the one in L.A., Dallas, Omaha, and finally Miami.

Miami was the smallest of all the firms, specializing in cases involving supernatural disputes. No one wanted to work there, least of all someone coming from the New York office. It made Wendy glad she'd quit when she did, or she'd be like the poor girl Michael had cheated on her with.

"Hello, can I help you?" an elderly woman with bubblegum-colored hair sat at a desk at the front of the office that Wendy could only assume was the receptionist.

"Yes, I have a complaint to file against a supernatural and was hoping to find someone who could help me get it to the right people."

"Do you have an appointment?" she looked down at an old-fashioned appointment calendar on top of her desk.

"No, I —" Wendy started but was interrupted by a squeal.

"Wendy? Is that really you?" the squeal belonged to the very person she had come to see.

Sage Spindle.

Ebony hair and caramel colored skin, the last time she had seen the woman she was being pounded into the copier by Michael, his face buried into her large breast. At the time all she had was anger and resentment toward her. Then when Nana told her about how he had tossed her aside as well, she realized all her anger should have been focused on the douche-bag and not on her ex-coworker who was just as much a victim as she had been.

"Yes, it's me." Wendy stepped around the desk, to offer Sage her hand but Sage just bypassed it, engulfing her in a tight hug.

"Oh my god, I swore I would die in this heat before I ever saw a New Yorker again. Not that you really are one being from England and all, but look, here you are!" Sage talked a-mile-a-minute, her hands animated in front of her the whole time.

"Yeah, here I am." She let her eyes take in the rest of the office behind her. There were only five desks including the secretary's, and besides them she hadn't seen another soul in the office. "Is this a slow time for you guys? I can come back if it's not."

"Ha!" Sage snorted. "A slow time, it's always a slow time, right, Beth?" She glanced over her shoulder at the nodding receptionist. "It's like they started this office and then forgot about it. I'm lucky to get enough cases to pay poor Bet's wages."

"You?" Wendy frowned. "You're the only one who works here?"

"Well, right now. The other girl, Sarah, is on maternity leave, so I've been covering her cases —what few there are and the random walkins every now and again." While she had a bright smile on her face, Wendy could see the strain around her eyes.

Just like Wendy, she had gone from an all-time high to an all-time low. It didn't make sense that they wouldn't keep the office fully staffed, she knew there were plenty of cases out there like her own. If what Sage was saying was true, Michael hadn't just given her an out. He'd fucked her over big time.

Righteous anger filled her and she shoved the paperwork over to Sage. "Well, consider me your newest client."

AFTER SHE FILLED Sage in on their case, they started talking about why the office didn't have many cases.

"It's marketing, I'm telling you," Wendy pointed out. "Do you think Michael and them just wait around for people to walk in?

No. They have teams around the clock spreading the word about the firm and how great they are."

"But we have a billboard and a radio commercial," Sage countered.

"Where is it? I didn't see it on my way here and when does this commercial play? You are in Florida now, not New York. People aren't up in the city all day. They are at the beach. You need to have prime placement for your advertisements and more than just one billboard that can easily be overlooked." Wendy started writing down the things the office needed to change.

"But I don't know how to do any of that stuff. Back in New York, they had someone who handled all that. I just did my cases and got new ones by referral, or from the higher ups." Sage's smile wilted a little bit as she realized the situation she was in.

"Well, you are here now, and you have to make the best of it. Unless you and Beth want to be out on the street, you need to find ways to get more clients." Looking around the empty office, Wendy tapped her lip with her pen. "It wouldn't hurt to get more lawyers in here that could bring their current clients with them and then some."

"What about you?" Sage gazed at her expectantly. "Where are you working right now?"

"Me?" Wendy placed a hand on her chest. "Nowhere at the moment. I'm still on vacation."

"See it's perfect!" Sage held her hands out to her. "You know all about the marketing stuff, and you're a great lawyer. With you on our payroll we'll get more clients in no time, I just know it!"

Wendy chewed on her lips, mulling it over. "I don't know, Sage, I haven't really figured out what I'm doing right now, and with the case against Peter, I'm not sure if I would be the best fit."

"Well, you don't have to answer now. Wait until after we get the rat bastard and then decide. Please?" Sage's lip stuck out in a pout, her eyes large and puppy dog like. Any man would be falling all over themselves to please her, and Wendy was hard-pressed not to say yes, right then and there.

"Fine. I'll think about it but no promises."

"Of course not! Thank you, thank you!" Sage jumped up from her seat, embracing Wendy as if she had already said yes. If she did end up working there, they would have to have a talk about personal space.

"Anyways, I have to get back to the ship and fill James in on what's going on. How long do you think it will take to get this before a judge?" She gestured to the papers on the desk.

"Oh, not long at all." Sage shook her head. "I might not have many clients, but one of the reasons I picked this area is because I have family here and three of them are judges right here in Miami."

Relieved to hear it, Wendy said her goodbyes and made her way back to the ship.

She was wondering if James was going to make good on his promise to spank her when she saw two large men in naval uniforms boarding the ship. What now?

# CHAPTER 18
## *JAMES*

IT WAS JUST his luck. He had a beautiful woman that he was sure he was truly on his way to being in love with, Pan was going to finally get what he deserved, and then all hell breaks loose.

The officers standing before him weren't anyone he knew, but they had the hard look of men who was used to tracking people down, and were good at it. They'd found him, and most people thought he was dead.

"Can I help you, gentlemen?" James placed his hands in his pockets and smiled at them. Nothing to see here. Move along.

"Yes, we are looking for a James Clocker, the captain of this vessel. Is that you?" One of the officers stepped forward, seeming to be of a higher rank.

"That depends on who is asking. What do you want with him?" He knew he was poking a snake.

With the military it was better just to answer their questions and go along with what they said. It was less painful for everyone involved. James couldn't do that. This time there was more at stake than just him going to prison. He had Wendy to think about, and Lily. That poor girl was so far gone he was lucky she hadn't bitten his hand off when he'd tried to feed her.

"Now that is classified information that can only be discussed with the man in question. So let's stop these games and answer the question. Are you James Clocker?" The officer asked the question again, this time a little less polite.

"Yeah, that'd be me." James pulled his hands out of his pockets and crossed his arms over his chest.

The other officer stepped toward him as the one in charge spoke, "Then by the authority of the U.S. military, you are hereby under arrest for the murder of twenty-six U.S. Naval soldiers.”

James was all ready to let them take him in, when the voice of an angel called out. “Wait!”

They all turned to look as Wendy came running up the ramp, her face flushed pink. Like a fiery angel, she swooped in between them, and stood in front of James, her hands on her hips.

“Ma’am, please step aside. This man is wanted for murder and should be considered dangerous.” The first officer tried to reason with her.

“First off, don’t ma’am me!” She pointed her finger at them. “Second, you said he was responsible for the deaths of twenty-six people, which leads me to believe you don’t know who this man actually is.”

The officers looked between her and then James. He just shrugged his shoulders and let his little hellion do her job.

“We have it on good authority from an eye witness that this man, James Clocker, killed our people when they went to investigate the new fae island. Now, are you telling me this is not the case?” He crossed his arms, showing he didn't believe anything she was saying.

"No, this is James Clocker. But this is also James Tinker, one of the so-called murder victims. Who also happens to be one of the prime witnesses for the case against the *fae* that killed your brothers and sisters." Wendy stepped toward the men, and James forced the smile off his face when they took a step back. "Now, wouldn't it seem counterintuitive to arrest him when he is the one helping to do your job?"

The two officers looked at each other and a silent conversation was exchanged in that moment. One that made James hold his breath as his fate was decided. But he shouldn't have worried, because the officer in charge focused back on them with a decisive look.

"Explain everything."

JAMES LET WENDY do all the talking. She seemed to know just what to say and had the soldiers in the palm of her hand before the hour was up.

"So, what proof do you have that this Peter Pan person is using magic against humans?" the officer in charge asked. He'd introduced himself as Officer Porter and his companion as Black. Not surprised by the lack of first names, James went with it.

"Well, besides James' story, and my own, we have come upon someone who is still under Peter's spell," Wendy explained, the confidence in her voice waning when it came to Lily. Though, it was her idea to kidnap the girl, she still seemed to have second thoughts.

"And where are they now?" Porter asked, his eyes searching around the deck of the ship.

"In my office," James stepped in. "We had to keep her out of sight in case Pan came for her. Plus she's not exactly in her right mind."

"Show us," Porter commanded as he gestured for them to lead the way.

He led them below deck and down to his office. Opening the door, he gestured them inside.

"Why is she tied up?" Black spoke up for the first time, his brow furrowed and a hard frown on his lips.

"Because, like I said she's not in her right mind. If we didn't restrain her she would find a way to get back to Pan," James explained, walking over to where Lily sat, her eyes glaring at the two new arrivals.

"I've never met someone under a sp—" Wendy clapped her hand over Black's mouth with a glare.

"Don't say that word!" Wendy hissed. "You can't tell her she's under one or she won't be able to get out of it. She has to figure it out on her own. That's the way it works."

She removed her hand from his mouth and moved over to where James stood. "She seems to have gotten better the longer she's away from him, but since James and I have both been in her position, it is easier for us to not mention it."

"So, you are going to use her to prove Pan's guilty?"

"No, you won't, you nasty leeches," Lily snarled. "I will not be used against my lover. He has done nothing wrong. You will pay for taking me away from him. Just you watch, he will rip your eyeballs from your skulls and feed it to his pet crocodile."

Before she could start rampaging, James grabbed the bit from his desk and shoved it into her mouth and looked at the soldiers. "See what I mean?"

"All right, we believe you." Porter strode up to the desk. "So how can we help?"

# CHAPTER 19
## *WENDY*

TRUE TO HER word, Sage had the case before a judge and them in court, not a week after Wendy had come to her. Officer Porter and Black ended up being a tremendous help by taking over Lily detail until it was time to go to court. Much to her and James' amusement, it seemed like Black was smitten with the bespelled girl, and demanded he be the one who brought her meals. He would sit beside her talking for hours.

"Good for her." James hugged Wendy tight to his side as they sat in the courtroom waiting for the judge to arrive.

"She has a long road ahead of her and she needs someone on her side."

"Yeah, but will he want to hang around for the person she will become once the spell is lifted?" Wendy tangled her hand in his, giving it a squeeze.

"Let's hope so—" Whatever he was going to say was cut off by the door to the courtroom opening. Peter Pan strolled in, a smug, shit-eating grin on his face. He didn't even seem worried that he was being charged with murder, rape, and multiple other infractions.

Coming in behind him was a petite blonde, her hair up in a sophisticated bun and wearing a green power suit. The moment she laid eyes on Wendy it was like razor blades to her heart. This woman had to be fae as well.

"Clocker, Wendy. How nice to see you again." Peter took a seat next to his lawyer, the deadly blonde, and leaned back in his chair as if he didn't have a care in the world.

Sage turned to Peter with a stern frown. "Please do not speak to my clients, you will have plenty of time to visit when you are behind bars."

Peter laughed and leaned toward her a seductive grin creeping up his face. "Now aren't you the most delectable creature I've ever seen. How would you like to come home with me after I'm found not guilty?"

The room got heavy for a moment and then whatever magic he had tried to perform evaporated as if sucked in by a black hole. This time Sage leaned into him with a nasty grin.

"Anti-magic charm." She pulled a circular pendant out of her blouse. "It wards against glamours and all other kinds of magical influence. So save your energy, because every public official has one after the incident with the President. Your kind have no place here."

It shocked Wendy to hear the sweet upbeat Sage sound so vicious by the very idea of magic or the fae in general. It would make working with her very interesting indeed, if Wendy decided to join the firm.

Peter slumped back in his chair, an annoyed look on his face. The blonde next to him tried to pat him on the back, but he shrugged her off with a frown.

"All rise for the honorable, Judge Hamilton," the bailiff announced to the room and a woman in her mid- to late-fifties took a seat at the judge's podium. Sage wasn't kidding when she said she knew a judge who could help them out. The woman could have been Sage's mother!

"You may be seated." Judge Hamilton glanced down at the papers before her. "Now, we are here because the plaintiffs believe that Mr. Pan here has used illegal magic on them, including the murder of twenty-five naval soldiers, attempted rape, and several other unimaginable crimes. Is this correct, counselor?" she directed her question towards Sage, who stood from her seat.

"That is correct, your honor." She nodded her head, taking a seat.

"And you Ms. Bell." Her eyes turned Pan's way. "How does your client plead?"

"Not guilty," the blonde said with a satisfied smile.

"Very well, because of the severity of this case and the nature of the defendant, we will get through this as quickly as possible so that the proper authorities can take over. Counselors, please present your opening statements."

NEVER HAVING BEEN on the client side, Wendy didn't realize how mind-numbing and anxiety-raking watching the lawyers do their work was. After Sage, and the one known as Ms. Bell, gave their opening statements, it was time to present the evidence. Which meant Wendy and James each had to tell their story to the whole courtroom.

Her story wasn't very long or as heartbreaking as James', so she had no problem going up to the stand. But once she was up there, and her eyes landed on Peter, who even though he couldn't use magic to sway the court, was just as smug as the moment he walked in.

"I was thankful enough to have come to my senses before Peter Pan could take advantage of me, but the damage he did to my mind will never be repaired." Wendy finished her explanation to Sage, who nodded her head.

"Thank you, Wendy, for sharing with us." Sage made her way back to her seat. "Your witness."

"Tell me, Wendy." The blonde stalked toward her a wicked gleam in her eye. "Did you not come to the Never Isles to have fun?"

"Yes," she stated plainly, not wanting to give her any ammunition.

"And didn't you expect, or even hope, to be swept away by some charming fae man who would make you forget your cheating ex-boyfriend?"

Frowning at the woman, Wendy chose her words carefully. "That was the expectation, yes."

"Then it seems to me, your honor," The blonde turned to the judge, "that what we have here is not a case of magical misuse, but a regretful slut calling foul once the deed is done."

"Objection!" Sage jumped from her seat.

"Sustained," the judge stated. "Ms. Bell, may I remind you, that name-calling will not be permitted in this courtroom."

"I apologize, your honor." She smirked at Wendy. "No further questions."

Wendy glared at Peter as she left the stand. He could be as pleased as he wanted. Just wait until their secret weapon showed up.

Wendy barely listened to James' story, but was proud that he was able to get through the whole thing without breaking down. Sage and Wendy had helped prepare him to go to the stand, making sure he tried to keep as true to the facts as possible since they didn't want any way for Peter and his lawyer to twist his words to their liking. Like with Wendy, it didn't help much.

"So, you are saying that you gunned down twenty-five of your fellow soldiers and you weren't responsible for any of it? It was the voice in your head making you do it?" Ms. Bell's face contorted into disbelief. "How do you even know that it was Peter Pan's magic that made you do it and not some kind of schizophrenic episode?" She turned to the jury. "It's not unheard of in our military for servicemen to have a mental breakdown. They do so much for this country and get so little in return, it is no wonder many of them eventually can't handle the stress."

"I am not insane!" James stood from his seat, pointing a finger at Peter. "He used his magic against me to kill my brothers and sisters. It is not something I would just make up to save my own hide!"

"And I'm sure Ted Bundy said the same thing." Bell put her hand up to her mouth with a grin. "Oops. I spoke out of place, your honor. I withdraw my last statement."

"Fine." The judge pursed her lips and then gestured to James. "You can step down from the stand." Shuffling her papers around on her podium, a frown creased her forehead. "Now, from what we have been presented it seems that all you have is the word of these two people against an upstanding gentleman who happens to be a member of the Council for Supernatural Creatures. Please tell me, counselor, you have more substantial proof than their word against his?"

"Of course, your honor." Sage motioned to the back of the courtroom where Porter stood waiting. Everyone turned to look at the courtroom door, where Black came in with Lily firmly against his side.

The moment she spotted Peter, though, she elbowed Black in the stomach and darted down the aisle. Peter's face was perfectly horrified as she came toward him, her arms outstretched and an adoring look in her eyes.

"Peter, my love. I waited for you. I tried to tell them that you'd be looking for me, and here you are!" Lily wrapped her arms around him, trying to kiss any part of him she could, but Peter wasn't having it.

He shoved her away and snarled, "Get away from me, you pathetic woman."

Lily wasn't deterred, instead she cocked her head to the side with a grin. "Are you grumpy today? Do you need your lily pad to take care of you?" To Wendy and she was sure everyone in the courtrooms shock, the girl dropped to her knees and tried to undo his pants.

"What is the meaning of this? Bailiff get her up." Judge Hamilton smacked her gavel against the counter.

The whole room had broken into chaos. Lily was insistent on giving Peter a blowjob, not caring who was watching. Peter and his blonde lawyer were trying to back away from her, denying knowing anything about the girl. Wendy was doing all she could not to start laughing at the sight they made.

"Somebody, get that girl out of here," the judge called out over the courtroom noise. "Quiet. Order in the courtroom. Order!"

"I think it would be best if I take it from here, your honor." All eyes turned to the back of the courtroom where a blonde woman, with ice blue eyes and a leather jacket, made her way down the aisle.

The moderator.

The moment Peter saw her, his panic at being caught turned to anger, and he launched himself across the room. Hands outstretched before him, he aimed for Wendy and James, not caring which one he got to first. Before he could lay a finger on them, green like vines shot out of the ground, wrapping around Peter's arms, legs, and mouth, leaving him squirming and screaming through the foliage.

Wendy stood from where she had ducked down, awe covering her face at the power of the moderator. She had seen her on television, but never in person, and never had she seen the kind of magic she had just performed.

"Moderator, you are just in time." The judge nodded at the blonde, who came to stand next to the restrained fae. "I believe no further action is needed on our part since the girl indeed proved he used magic against at least one of these humans."

"Yes, the council will take it from here. There will be a thorough investigation into every human he has ever encountered. And don't worry, he won't be able to hide anything from us." She smirked and gave the bundle of green a thump.

"Miss Moderator, thank you so much. You saved our lives." Wendy clutched James to her, not believing it was finally over.

The blonde woman shrugged her shoulders, seeming a bit embarrassed by the praise. "Just doing my job."

# CHAPTER 20
## *JAMES*

WITH PAN TAKEN to the fae courts to be tried for his crimes, life had kind of gone back to normal for James. Well as normal as it could be.

Black and Porter said they would report back to the base about what happened with Pan, and would be in touch with him about a possible reinstatement of his military position. James wasn't sure whether or not he would take it. He kind of liked being a sea captain. And now that he wasn't limited to just the Never Isles, it would be nice to go somewhere else for a change.

"Where are you going to go?" Wendy asked one night as he held her in his arms after a long bout of lovemaking.

"Well, I've been on that island for about eight years, my family probably thinks I'm dead, so I would like to go see them. Put the record straight."

"And where it that?" Her voice was low and even, as if trying not to show any emotion.

"Upstate New York actually." He smoothed a hand down her bare back, watching the reaction on her face.

"But what about the Jolly Roger? Who's going to take care of it? And your clients?"

"Oh, I'm bringing her with me, of course. I can't leave Smith in charge. He'd have her run to ground before I left the state." They both laughed at his poking at the older man.

"Will you call me when you are there?" She worried her bottom lip, the way she did when she was struggling to find her words.

"What do you mean call you? You're coming with me, aren't you? I have to introduce my girlfriend to my parents."

James cupped her face in his hands. "I mean, that is if you want to come."

Wendy's mouth spread out into a huge smile, and all of a sudden, she jumped into his arms, kissing every inch of his face. "Of course, I want to come!"

"Really?" he pulled her down to look her in the eyes.

"Silly pirate, don't you know I've been crazy about you since the moment you spanked my ass?" Her face flushed at the memory.

"Made an impression on you, did I?" James pulled her into his lap, his hands caressing her bare cheeks, but before he could get one swing in, she pushed out of his arms.

"Wait!"

"What is it? What's wrong?" His brow furrowed in confusion.

"What about Sage? I can't just leave her high-and-dry after I agreed to help her get the firm back on its feet." She jumped from the bed and began looking for her clothes.

"But didn't you just hire two others to help around there? Can't she spare you for a week or two?" He slipped from the bed, coming up behind her.

"I guess, maybe," she muttered. "I could probably just work from the road, you know. I mean, we'll have to get WiFi for the ship, but I think I could probably make it work. Though, I am kind of reluctant to leave right now."

"Why's that?"

"You should have seen the guy that came in today. Poor Sage was smitten the moment she saw him, but if you heard his story you'd understand." Wendy smiled up at him with a twinkle in her eye. "It's too bad she hasn't figured out he's a fae, yet. I'm sure once she does there will be drama all over the place."

"Well, why don't you tell me all about it." James said, pulling her into his arms. "After our bath."

Giggling at his antics, she let him carry her to the bathroom, where more fun awaited. "As you command, Captain."

# About the Author

Erin Bedford is an otaku, recovering coffee addict, and Legend of Zelda fanatic. Her brain is so full of stories that need to be told that she must get them out or explode into a million screaming chibis. Obsessed with fairy tales and bad boys, she hasn't found a story she can't twist to match her deviant mind full of innuendos, snarky humor, and dream guys.

On the outside, she's a work from home mom and bookbinger. One the inside, she's a thirteen-year-old boy screaming to get out and tell you the pervy joke they found online. As an ex-computer programmer, she dreams of one day combining her love for writing and college credits to make the ultimate video game!

Until then, when she's not writing, Erin is devouring as many books as possible on her quest to have the biggest book gut of all time. She's written over thirty books, ranging from paranormal romance, urban fantasy, and even scifi romance.

www.erinbedford.com
Facebook.com/erinrbedford
twitter.com/erin_bedford

9 781951 958411